Bishop
as
Pawn

BISHOP
AS
PAWN

by
Ralph McInerny

FATHER DOWLING
Mystery

THE VANGUARD PRESS
NEW YORK

For Rog and Lou and Ray and Jean

Bishop
as
Pawn

1

MARIE MURKIN, peering out through a filigree of frost on the window of her kitchen door at St. Hilary's rectory, could not believe her eyes. She actually stepped away from the door and threw up her hands as if to ward off all the ghosts and goblins of a long ago childhood: faces descried on winter window-panes, voices heard in the wind, footsteps in the creaks of joists and beams.

The tapping repeated itself. A branch brushing the house? Marie flicked on the porch light and, through two panes of glass and fifteen years, looked out at Billy. When he smiled, actually smiled, she could have screamed. But what she did was to open both doors and let him in.

"It's cold out there."

She stared at him in disbelief. How dare he be so casual? "How did you find me?"

"Were you lost?" His wry ironic grin disarmed her. He stood there, taller than she remembered, thin, hugging himself. Well, he always had. Why did she feel on the defensive?

"Was *I* lost!"

"Where would I find you except in a church, or . . ." His eyes traveled insolently around the room and his brow rose in appraisal.

"Get out of here."

"Now, Marie, you know I'm only kidding."

Kidding? The man was beyond belief. He made her want to scream, to laugh, to beat him with her fists. She hated him. It seemed to her that she had always hated him. He had turned her life into one of his unfunny jokes: the man who steps out for a package of cigarettes and is gone for fifteen years. Fifteen years during which she had rehearsed what she would say to him if they ever met again on this side of the grave. As for the other side, well, he would find a sterner judge than Marie Murkin there. And now here he was and he had somehow gotten the advantage of her and she could not remember any of the devastating unanswerable accusations she had prepared on sleepless lonely nights, speaking to the ceiling above her bed as if it represented both God and Billy Murkin.

She sank into a kitchen chair and began to sob helplessly. Her small body convulsed and shook. He put his hand on her shoulder, tentatively at first, then more firmly. Finally, he drew her against him and put his arms awkwardly about her.

"There, there," he said, his hand making a circular motion between her shoulder blades. That motion awakened a memory she had not known she had. Is the flesh imprinted with the past, needing only a touch to bring it out, as heat brings out from paper messages written there in lemon juice?

The buzzer of the oven went off and Marie scrambled

to her feet. She had a supper to get ready. She had responsibilities. Billy watched her remove the cake and turn off the oven, leaving the door ajar so that more heat was added to the room.

"Where are you staying?" she asked, not looking at him.

"I just got in."

From where? How? Why? She did not want to know. "You can't stay here."

"Marie!" He looked at her as if she had made an indecent suggestion.

"In case you thought you could." She turned away to a cupboard.

"Do you live here?"

"How did you find me?"

When she turned to him again, she wanted to stare; she wanted to study this man who had turned her life into a ruin. Did she really hate him? She certainly did not love him. She could not believe that she had ever loved him, with his wide mouth and weak merry eyes. Beyond passion and feeling, she would simply like to study him and find out what made him the monster he was.

"You're in the phone book."

"I am not."

"Well, the rectory is."

"How did you know I was here?"

She had been here for years, almost since he had gone, cooking and cleaning for the priests. She had seen pastors come and go. The current pastor, Father Dowling, was the first in years who seemed permanent. Father Dowling! How was she going to explain to him that her husband had shown up at the kitchen door after an absence of fifteen years and was now settling himself at the table and lighting a cigarette?

"Got an ashtray, Marie?"

She glared at him. Is this what people talked about after so long a separation? Billy blew smoke toward the ceiling and held out an expired match, fastidiously, between thumb and forefinger. She put a saucer before him.

"Use that. And for heaven's sake, take off your coat."

"Where is everybody?"

"What do you mean?"

"The priests." He mouthed the word theatrically. "I came to the back door to avoid them."

"There's only one. The pastor."

She imagined Billy coming to the front door and being met by Father Dowling. What would he have said to the priest? How would he have asked for her? Marie was swept by embarrassment. She had told Father Dowling about Billy, in a guarded way, not going into detail. It was scarcely a feather in her cap and she had not wanted to dwell on it. Over the years she had become the efficient reliable housekeeper of St. Hilary's, her attitude toward parishioners almost clerical, even condescending, as if she represented some standard they were failing to meet. What a façade that now seemed! What would Father Dowling think when he saw the husband who had deserted her fifteen years ago?

2

IN A FRONT parlor of the house, Roger Dowling looked across his desk at Eunice Flanagan who for the second time had failed to bring with her the boy she meant to marry.

"He's never met a priest," she said, the explanation accompanied by an apologetic smile. "I think he's a little afraid."

"Would it help if I met him somewhere else than here?"

"No. No, you don't have to do that."

"We could meet for coffee somewhere, perhaps for lunch, the three of us."

"I'll bring him here, Father. I promise."

She made it sound like something he demanded of her. He knew the range of fears and suspicions the non-Catholic can harbor toward a priest, knew too that, as often as not, they were easily dissipated. Nowadays, of course, it was difficult to tell a priest from anyone else, but Roger Dowling doubted that beards and turtlenecks and tweed jackets were the best bridge across the chasm of distrust. He at any rate still wore traditional clerical dress.

"Of what religion is he, Eunice?"

"Oh, it isn't that."

"What do you mean?"

"He hasn't any. He's just nothing. Nothing at all."

"I see. Then you've talked about it."

"Yes."

"And how did he react? Was he hostile, interested, what?"

She thought about that, bringing a finger to her lips as if to stay any comment until she had given it thought. With her ginger hair and freckled face she was a parody of an Irish colleen, pretty, pixyish, in her early twenties. Her family did not live in St. Hilary's parish, nor did she, as it turned out. He had assumed she did, when she first called and asked if she might come see him with her fiancé. Twice she had come and he had yet to meet the young man. Was it possible that he did not exist?

"He's just not interested," Eunice said finally.

"Hostile?

"He's against it, against organized religion. He says it's all a matter of money."

Dowling glanced at the index card on the desk before him, at the name he had written there next to Eunice's. Andrew Pilsen.

"What is his family like?"

"I don't know."

"They don't live in Fox River?"

She shook her head. Did she know where they lived?

Dowling was unable to shake the vagrant thought that Eunice was telling him of a fictitious fiancé. Surely she had no need for fantasy. She seemed pretty enough, fully capable of attracting young men, young Catholic men, for the matter of that, thus avoiding the complications of her engagement to Andrew Pilsen.

"Well," he said, sighing and placing his hands on the desk. "We really can't do anything without him. You know the Church's view on marriage, I imagine. It is the young man who will have to be instructed."

"You mean, no divorce?"

"That and other things. More positive things."

"Andrew says all it takes is money. He claims that all kinds of people, Catholics, get divorces because they can afford to pay for them."

Dowling smiled. As a veteran of years on the marriage tribunal of the Archdiocese of Chicago, he had met many who could have afforded an annulment if all it took was money. Perhaps there was some truth to the charge, perhaps only those with money could afford the lengthy litigation. But the real cost was patience, and the almost certain prospect of refusal, and few are rich in patience.

"He does sound hostile. I'd like to meet him."

"He'll argue with you."

"No doubt. I should think he'd welcome a chance to confront the enemy."

"He's against so many things," Eunice said, frowning past Dowling at a bookshelf. "It's as if everything is corrupt and he knows it and the rest of us ignore it." Her voice trailed off. It was not the tone of a girl in love.

"Has he met your parents?"

"My mother."

"But not your father?"

"Not yet. My mother told me I should talk with you. With a priest." Eunice put her arms into the sleeves of the coat she had draped over her chair. "I think she hopes you'll talk me out of it."

"Did she try to talk you out of it?"

Coat on, standing, Eunice said, "In a way. She reminded me that marriage is for keeps, that it is a sacrament, that mixed marriages have special problems."

"She's right, you know."

"I know. I guess I know." She smiled, bravely. It seemed to Roger Dowling that the room had grown gloomy as they sat there. Getting up from his chair, he walked Eunice to the street door.

"Eunice, I want to meet your Andy. Perhaps I could phone him and . . ."

"No." She put a hand on his arm. "No, I'll talk to him. I'll arrange it. And I am sorry I didn't bring him today."

"That's all right."

"I'll call you," she said, and then she was striding toward the curb where her Pacer was parked in the slushy street, its windows steamed, looking vaguely like a spaceship.

The snow was somewhat unseasonable for late March, heavy, wet; it clung to branches like suds and the trees looked blacker for their burden of snow. The street lights were already on and from a distance the roar of the traffic on the Interstate was audible. Roger Dowling remained at the front door after Eunice Flanagan had driven away and there was a pensive expression on his face.

He had learned from a typewritten history of the parish compiled by his predecessor that he was the seventh pastor of St. Hilary's in Fox River, Illinois. Despite his age, he was relatively new to pastoral work. For most of the quarter century of his priesthood he had worked on the archdiocesan marriage tribunal, specializing in the misery of others, trying to make the map of canon law conform to the crazy contours created by living human agents. Litigation is often a protest against personal responsibility, a refusal to accept the consequences of one's own free choices. Disenchanted spouses wondered why, thirty or thirty-five years afterward, they should be saddled with the promises made by earlier versions of themselves, some callow youth or naive maid who could not possibly have known what he or she was getting into. So erase the past, deny its promises, and assume that, in the present, one is capable of doing what that earlier version of the self could not do. One marriage annulled in order that another might be contracted. No legal code, or interpretation of it, could meet such demands. Not even God can undo what has been done. Dowling had aged and anguished in the job, carrying its burden in silence until it had brought him down. He had begun to drink. The habit came upon him almost unawares, in middle life, though when it came it seemed predestined. The Irish weakness. There had been relatives, an uncle, several cousins; he should have known. It was in the blood. He had been marked for clerical advancement but the drinking ruled that out and he ground on at the marriage court, noted for conscientiousness and for his ability to stave off despair when everyone else had given up hope.

He read his Dante almost as regularly as his breviary and no longer thought of those who came before the tribunal as anomalies, out of the mainstream of believers whose lives were successful, happy, embodiments of the ideal. He recognized that the broken souls he dealt with *were* the mainstream, and so was he with his tendency to pity and pardon where blame perhaps was in order. The only one he could not spare was himself. A final epic binge, a cure, and then, as though into exile, he had been sent to St. Hilary's in Fox

River, a city west of Chicago. Fifty years of age, a failure in the eyes of many of his friends, he had come to see this parish as his sweetest consolation. God is merciful.

So Eunice's strange fiancé caused him concern. He did not want her to stumble into a marriage that was destined to end up one day before the archdiocesan marriage tribunal. He was going to have to speak to Andrew Pilsen.

3

ANDY PILSEN was going bald at twenty-five and he did not like it at all. Not that he did anything about it. The thought of falling for one of those sucker ads that promised to stimulate the follicles with ointments or vibrators or radiation made him laugh. He read such come-ons whenever he found one and, despite himself, he would feel hope stir in his breast, but the truth was that he could not have afforded a treatment even if he had been able to persuade himself that it was worth it. A wig? Zinnia who worked the bar with him wore a wig. Of course everyone told him it looked great, the customers, Zinnia's wife, Andy himself; what the hell, why break Zinnia's heart, but the truth was that the damned thing stuck out in back like a bird's tail and looked phoney even in the dim light of the bar. As for outside, in the daylight, forget it. What Andy would have done, if he could have afforded it, was go for the plug treatment, the Sinatra and Senator Proxmire route, transplant hair from the chest or armpit, real hair and his own. But he had seen pictures of Frankie and Proxmire that suggested that not even transplants would fool anyone. It made more sense to notice guys who looked good bald, who accepted it gracefully, guys you couldn't even imagine with hair on their heads. The trouble with this was that he did not look remotely like any bald man whose baldness looked okay.

No one would have suspected Andy of thinking much about his hair or the growing absence of it. He washed what remained infrequently, he wore it long, he parted it exactly in the middle even though the part was now two inches wide and bordered by scarcely visible, thinning strands. He had worn it to his shoulders until some customer, watching a biblical movie on the television set above the bar, had pointed to the screen and said, "Hey, Andy. That's you. One of the apostles."

By the time he turned, the scene had changed and he never did get a look at the actor who had reminded the customer of Andy Pilsen. Later he asked Zinnia if he had been watching the TV at the time.

"Yeah, sure."

"You see the guy supposed to look like me?"

Zinnia nodded in the deliberate way that suggested he was afraid his hairpiece would slip off and land on the bar.

"What'd he look like?"

Zinnia squinted at him. "Like you. Know what I mean? You heard the customer. He looked like you."

He should have known better than to ask. It was Zinnia who had said that the limes they used for gin and tonic smelled like aftershave. But it was the fact that his lookalike

had been an apostle that led Andy, to get his hair cut short·
well, shorter: it still covered his ears.

"Use a dryer," Eunice had said "After you wash it,
use a dryer."

"A dryer! Are you kidding?"

"Lots of men use them."

"Tell me about it."

"On television. In the ads."

If television commercials were her idea of the real
world, he had his work cut out for him. The joke was that she
had finished college, graduating from Rosary with a major in
history, and he had less than two years total when he counted
up the credits he had earned in five different institutions over
a span of six years. He told people he had gone to Chicago,
knowing they would assume he meant the university, but his
college life, such as it was, had been spent in a variety of
community and junior colleges no one would have heard the
names of. Which was just as well. Most high schools were more
demanding than those places. The only good professor he ever
had was indicted in the middle of the quarter for violating
one of the more arcane laws of the commodity market. The
man must have spent most of his day on his investments, he
had brokers in New York as well as Chicago and he had been
briefly worth over a million dollars. On paper. He had been
wiped out when his margins were called, whatever that meant.
Andy Pilsen sure as hell did not know. He had been shocked
by the news. The course had been in Greek Ethics and
Quellen, the professor, had been eloquent in his exposition of
the Nicomachean Ethics. Pilsen, desperately curious about a
vision of human life untainted by religion, had thought he
found in Aristotle a pagan after his own heart. Quellen had
taken them through the arguments against false views of happiness: pleasure, power, honor, wealth. They had been demol-
ishing the view that wealth is productive of human happiness

when Quellen's indictment hit the papers with the story of how he had spent his day, on the phone to his brokers, adding to his portfolio, deep in grain and cattle futures. The next class Quellen told them a long anecdote about how Thales had cornered the olive presses to show that a philosopher could make money if he chose to. Of course the point of the story was that the philosopher chose not to, which made Quellen something other than a philosopher. Aristotle was never the same again.

Zinnia had been impressed when Andy told him the story

"My God, ask his advice. Get a stock we should buy. Tha guy must really know the market."

'He lost everything, Zinnia Read the story."

'He had to make it to lose it, didn't he? How many people you know who've lost a million dollars?"

"One."

Eunice said, "There's nothing wrong with money, Andy. You take money for tending bar, don't you?"

"Not very much."

"Why do you do it? You could get a better job."

"I like the hours."

She thought he was kidding, but it was true. He liked to have the day hours to himself. He came on at six and worked until two in the morning which was as early as he was likely to get to bed anyway and he could sleep till noon if he wanted to.

Eunice used his hours as an excuse for putting off the visit to the priest. The priest was busy in the afternoon when Andy could have gone to see him. Well, she had better set it up soon. It was bad enough that her parents were against the marriage, because Andy had no religion; they didn't know any better. But no priest was going to stand between Andrew Pilsen and his girl.

4

WHEN she left Father Dowling, Eunice drove slowly through the slushy streets, more out of reluctance to go home than because of the driving conditions. Her slowness angered other drivers and several times she was honked at from behind and then passed by a driver with an enraged expression. She had half a mind to return their imagined profanities as they went by. What was the rush? Where was everybody going in such a hurry?

The rear of her car swung to the left when she slowed at an intersection, but she let up on the brake, spun the wheel and got the car straightened out before once more slowing it. When she had come to a full stop, she sat staring at the red traffic signal through the rhythmic sway of the windshield wiper and realized that she had been frightened by the sliding of her car. It was a good day for accidents. A bad day. But what day is not? She imagined herself being struck broadside, thrown from her car, carried away to the hospital in an ambulance whose wailing siren would be the last sound she would ever hear. DOA. She smiled. The thought of just ceasing to be was almost attractive.

But God was on the other side of death. He was on this side too, but where? She addressed Him in prayer, she visited Him in church, she was constantly aware of His eye upon her, but He was not the kind of observer she could turn and see. She knew what He thought of her affair with Andrew.

Affair. She preferred the old-fashioned word; it lent some dignity to the time they spent in the bed in his jumbled room. Each visit, she spent half the time picking things up and putting them away. Andrew told her to forget it, it didn't matter, but she could not stand disorder and squalor. Besides, being busy kept her from thinking of why they had come to this weird room at the top of a warehouse that Andrew called his apartment. She hated the messiness of the place, she found his indifference to cleanliness repellent. Then why? Why? He was the first man she had ever slept with and the only way she could justify it was to pretend that they were going to marry. She had expected Andrew to reject the idea when she brought it up, had thought she was providing him with an excuse to drop her, but he seized upon it as if it had been his own idea.

"What will we live on?" she asked.

"I've got a job, you've got a job."

"You want me to go on working?"

"For a while, sure. Why not?"

"Where will we live?"

He had looked around his vast room which he persisted in calling an apartment. It did have a bath and there was a kitchen in a corner, but it was only one room, no matter how large, and the most prominent object of furniture was the bed. She had felt that the first time she went there. The place was like a stage and in its center was the bed and the audience would know what sort of scene was about to be played. The audience, of course, was God.

"God! You're kidding."

Andrew, naked beside her, she could not bear to look at him, propped himself on an elbow and stared at her with a strange off-center grin.

"I'm Catholic."

He shook his head. He laughed once, unconvincingly, then stared at her some more.

"Eunice, look, I don't want to hurt your feelings, believe me, but you can't really believe . . ."

"Not believe. I know." She did not want to argue about it. Somehow she was not surprised to learn that he was an atheist. What else would he be? Living the way he did.

To sleep with an atheist made the act more degrading than it would otherwise have been, and also less real. It involved her less. She knew that sex is sacred, that it belonged only in marriage. And she also knew that it had to be a great deal more than what she had just shared with Andrew. Her curiosity had made her vulnerable to his obvious and inept approach. She had stopped with another girl at the bar where he worked and he had pestered them to death, ignoring the other customers, coming on strong. It was when Irene whispered that he was really good-looking that Eunice had taken an interest in him. She gave him her name and phone number and during the next few days actually longed for him to call. He was unlike any boy she had known. They had treated her with respect. At most, they had tried to fondle her breasts. Once a boy had inched his hand up beneath her skirt and she had closed her eyes, not wanting him to do that, not wanting him to stop either, and her tension had shamed him and he withdrew his hand and apologized and she never saw him again. Irene heard that he had told someone he was unworthy of Eunice Flanagan. She knew that she was called the Blessed Virgin.

Andrew telephoned and there was no danger that he would be reluctant to take whatever he could, so they had gone to bed and it had been a whole lot less than she had expected, and she had not felt remorse until she was home again in her own bed. That was when she had decided she would tell Andrew they had to get married, not had to, but they must, and he would scuttle off and that would be that. Only he liked the idea and she had to put him off by saying that her parents opposed it and then, another trump, by saying that he would have to go talk to the priest.

She had not known Father Dowling previously. She did not live in St. Hilary's parish. But from the first time she saw him, she felt certain that Father Dowling would tell her how to free herself from Andrew. Of course she had not told him yet precisely what the problem was. She did not want to marry Andrew Pilsen. Would she actually have to bring Andrew to see Father Dowling so the priest could see the kind of man he was and prevent her from marrying him?

Andrew had been furious when, without crossing her fingers, she told him that Father Dowling was adamantly opposed to their marriage.

5

"FATHER, Billy's here. My husband, Billy Murkin."

Marie stood in the doorway of Roger Dowling's study, a strange smile on her face, her manner nervous, her voice quavering. Behind her, blocked from view except for a long face with a sheepish expression, stood a man.

"Billy?" Dowling pushed back from his desk, confused. Marie was Mrs. Murkin but she had never mentioned her husband before except as a figure in the dim past. Once he had said something that suggested she was a widow and been corrected, but without further explanation.

"He's back." She stepped aside so that Dowling could see him. It might have been a magic act. Billy, the rabbit produced, came across the room with outstretched hand. Dowling shook it.

"Well, well." He looked to Marie for help. "Back from where?"

"Oh," Billy said and grinned. His hand went out in an arc. "Everywhere."

"Father, it's been fifteen years."

Dowling sat down and stared at Marie and then at her resurrected husband. Fifteen years! There seemed nothing at all to say that was not better left unsaid.

"Of course he won't be staying here, Father."

Marie's room was in the back of the house, on the second floor, reached by a private stairway. Dowling had no idea how large her room might be, but then he was not sure why Marie insisted that Billy would not be staying in the house. Did she imagine that he would object?

"You're certainly welcome to stay," he said, but Marie interrupted with a cry.

"No! No, he doesn't want to. He just stopped by."

"After fifteen years?" There was no way he could stop the question. To his relief, Billy found it funny. He laughed, an odd barking sound, but his glance at Marie suggested something less than aplomb.

"I wasn't looking for a place to stay," Billy said, but he seemed to be taking the measure of the room and his eyes drifted to the ceiling. One of the unused curate rooms? Dowling was not about to suggest that. Billy had the look of a likable irresponsible drifter. If he stayed in the house it would have to be with Marie. After all, they were, presumably, man and wife. If Dowling had not known her better, he might have wondered if his housekeeper was trying to introduce a paramour into the house under false pretenses. But Marie was clearly less eager to shelter Billy than Father Dowling was.

"Indeed you're not," she said firmly. She took his arm and tugged him toward the doorway. "You go back to the kitchen while I have a word with Father Dowling."

When he had gone, Marie shut the door and turned a desolate face to the priest.

"He just walked in. After fifteen years."

"I'm surprised you recognized him."

"He hasn't changed. Not a bit. He's older, that's all. Father, what will I do?"

"Marie, I haven't the faintest idea. He is still your husband?"

"Yes." She wailed the word.

"I meant it when I said he could stay."

But she shook her head, furiously, the tears bright in her eyes. Roger Dowling felt that he had made a gauche suggestion and he backed swiftly away from the apparent subject of this incredible exchange.

"Marie, I leave it all to you."

"But what am I going to do?"

It was a question, whatever theoretical answers there might be to it, best left to poor Marie. What rights did a husband gone for fifteen years retain? Roger Dowling was surprised that Marie had even let the man into the house. Had she been pining for him all these years, unconsciously awaiting his knock on the door? And now he was here and she did not know what to do.

"Where's he been?" Phil Keegan asked later that night.

"I don't know."

"Didn't he say?"

"He didn't say anything to me. Why should he? What did you make of him?"

Keegan shrugged, but Dowling thought he recognized a professional interest on the part of the Fox River chief of detectives.

"I hope you don't think he's using my rectory for a hideout."

"No, Roger. He's your kind of problem, not mine."

That was a remark Phil no doubt would have liked to take back some hours later when the body of Billy Murkin was carried down the back stairs from the housekeeper's room and driven away to the morgue. Nor was Keegan's disposition improved by the medical examiner's estimate of the time of death. However inexact his guess, it was inescapable that Billy Murkin had been fatally shot while Phil Keegan and Roger Dowling were playing chess in the rectory office.

They were still playing when Marie's scream lifted both men from their chairs. She seemed to be falling downstairs and screaming at the same time. Keegan ran down the hallway to the kitchen and reached the back stairs just as Marie burst into the kitchen. The hulking figure of the policeman did not calm her; indeed, when Phil reached to support her, she became hysterical. Phil slapped her, sat her down in a chair, crouched before her and demanded to know what was the matter. But all she could do was point toward the stairs, her eyes rolling in her head.

Dowling followed Keegan up the stairs to the chintzy surprise of Mrs. Murkin's quarters. Billy was sprawled across the bed, his head a bloody mess. Knowing it was too late, Dowling said the prayer of absolution. Billy lay on his face. Behind him, the window was shattered. Keegan was scowling at the glass all over the floor.

"Even with a silencer, we should have heard the window."

"A silencer?"

"Did you hear a shot?"

Dowling walked to the window and peered out into the snowy night. Keegan pulled him to one side.

"They may still be out there."

"They?"

"Whoever." Keegan picked up the phone beside the

bed and called downtown. Meanwhile, Roger Dowling went to comfort Marie Murkin. In the course of a few hours, she had become once more a wife, just in time to become a widow. She sobbed silently now, staring vacantly ahead. Dowling poured a drink from the bottle of brandy he kept for Phil Keegan. He had to help Marie get it down. She was in a state of shock, and no wonder. When he put his hand on her shoulder, she lurched away, looking wildly around. Dowling was happy to hear the heavy tread of Phil Keegan descending the stairs.

"They're on their way. Mrs. Murkin . . ." He stopped when Dowling gestured. Phil addressed the priest. "Better get someone to look after her. She sure isn't going to spend to-night upstairs."

Dowling wondered if she would ever want to stay there again. The prospect of St. Hilary's without Marie Murkin loomed gloomily.

"Is he dead? Is he dead?" She addressed the question wildly, first to Keegan, then to Dowling.

"He's dead," Keegan told her.

"The last sacraments," Marie pleaded, tugging at Dowling's sleeve.

"It's been done. I gave him absolution."

"Oh, thank God. Thank God."

Keegan nodded in embarrassed acquiescence. "When exactly did you find him, Mrs. Murkin?"

But it was a mistake to think that she was ready to talk about it. At that moment, sirens became audible and soon the house was swarming with Keegan's colleagues. Marie sat crumpled at her kitchen table, using a dish towel for a hand-kerchief, following the proceedings with dread curiosity. Dowling got her out of the kitchen before they brought the body down. Mrs. Hanson, a bit of a pest but good as gold, had by then arrived, in answer to Dowling's summons. She had been halfway to the parish house, coming to see what all the commotion was about, when one of her kids came calling her back to the phone. Thus, the formal request that she come had delayed her arrival.

"I think the rectory's on fire," she said breathlessly, when she came to the phone. "Where are you, Father?"

"I'm in the rectory, Mrs. Hanson. There's no fire. It's something else. Mrs. Murkin's husband is dead."

"Her husband?"

"Yes. I wondered if you could come look after her. She is taking it rather badly."

Mrs. Hanson's voice made it clear that wild horses could not keep her away now and Roger Dowling wondered if she had been the right person to call. The fact that he had thought of her first suggested that she was. There was, however, a tense moment when Mrs. Murkin looked up and saw Mrs. Hanson in her kitchen, but soon the two women were embracing, both weeping so that it was impossible to tell which was the widow and which the consoler. It seemed safe for Dowling and Keegan to return to the study.

"What have they learned?"

"Upstairs? They've hardly started. Not that they'll find anything. What interests me is outside the house."

"Well?"

"The ramp leading up to the Interstate."

"But that's blocks away."

"Not quite five hundred yards as the bullet flies. It was the obvious place, on a direct line from the window and at approximately the same height."

"Good Lord."

The thought of that sniper in the night was difficult to get rid of and later, when they had finished in Marie's room and Phil Keegan too had gone, Roger Dowling, in his own room, lights out, stood at his window and stared out into the night. He could see the lights that illuminated the ramp from which the shot had come but not the ramp itself. His own window would not be visible from it, because of a group of chestnut trees in a yard that intervened between the ramp and house.

A sniper's bullet: it seemed as judgmental as a bolt of lightning, an act of God, violence coming out of the soft snowy night, unexpected, mortal. Had Billy Murkin any inkling that this might happen? Had he been fleeing his assassin, the fear of death bringing him back to the wife he had deserted fifteen years ago?

One thing seemed clear. Phil Keegan was going to be very interested in those lost fifteen years.

PHIL KEEGAN was not the kind of cop who feels apologetic about the law, as if perhaps it is those who abide by it rather than those who transgress it who belong in jail. He had been told that ours is an imperfect society, that certain injustices are institutionalized within it. This seemed to mean that some had more money than others. Keegan could not conceive of any alternative to this arrangement that made any sense to him. In any case, wealth is not a pot of gold already there from which unequal portions are taken by the finders. The people Keegan knew who had money, with exceptions of course, had come by it through their own sweat and effort. Had Bill Flanagan, who built a little sheet-metal shop into one of the biggest construction firms in Fox River, taken the money he now had from the pockets of the poor? There would be a lot more empty pockets if it had not been for Bill Flanagan.

Flanagan came into his thoughts because that is where Marie Murkin's long gone husband had worked.

"In Fox River?" Father Dowling, lighting his pipe, looked across the flame at Keegan.

"He was living not two miles from this rectory, Roger."

"During all that time?"

"Well, he was at that address for twelve years. The search goes on." He glared at Dowling to make certain that the priest knew that final remark was parody.

"It reminds me of a story by Nathaniel Hawthorne," Dowling mused. "But surely, Phil, if he lived right here in town, if he had a phone . . ."

"He changed his name."

"But people would recognize him."

It turned out that the assumptions Dowling was making were unfounded, but Keegan had had to question Marie Murkin to learn this. Marie was both anxious to get out of Mrs. Hanson's house and fearful of returning to her room at the rectory. It said something of Mrs. Hanson that Marie chose her own room rather than stay on at the Hansons to whose home a steady stream of parish stalwarts came, to inquire about Marie, to get a look at her, to find out from Flo Hanson the latest speculation.

Marie seemed almost relieved to be questioned by Keegan, a familiar figure to her because of his friendship with Father Dowling and his frequent visits to the rectory. And, as one who had complimented her cooking many times, more a friend than an official.

"How long had you been married to Billy, Marie?"

The ring she twisted on her finger must have been her wedding ring. "We married three years before we came here, to Fox River." She inhaled deeply and let her breath out slowly. "We were married for nineteen years. We lived in Fox River a year before he left me."

"Tell me about that."

"What do you mean?"

"Why did he go? What brought it on? Was it a quarrel, drink, a woman?"

Marie smiled sadly. "All of them. Things had been nice enough the first three years. It was coming here, to a strange city where we knew no one, that ruined him."

He let her go on, visualizing Marie as a young woman, still newly married in a way, for whom Fox River had been a large city compared with the town from which they came. Keegan could not help but think of his own marriage, of his wife, now dead, of the sweet long ago. He shook these thoughts away. Sympathetic as he might be with Marie Murkin, he did not welcome the notion they had much in common. His loneliness did not crave company. The difficult part of the interview still lay ahead.

"Where did he go when he left, Marie?"

"I don't know."

"Did you discuss that at all, when he came back, before it happened?"

She looked desolate. "Captain Keegan, that is the worst thing, in a way. I was so busy fixing supper. Father had company coming. You. And Billy was just in the way so, after I'd given him something to eat, I told him to go upstairs. Just to wait there. I wanted him out from under my feet."

"I understand."

"Well, after I'd served and cleaned up and had a bite myself, I went upstairs and Billy was . . ."

With what hopes and expectations, with what anger, had she trudged up those stairs, tired at the end of her day, to confront the husband who had left her all those years ago? Had there been other emotions too, hope, even desire? The thought was uncharacteristic for Keegan, but he found the image of Marie Murkin going up those stairs to see Billy an indelible one.

"He was dead," Keegan said. She was going to have to use the word, there is no adequate substitute for it. Besides, she was a woman of faith, and whatever Billy had been, Dowling had given him conditional absolution. Keegan sometimes pondered that people of the kind Billy apparently had been, who got by by the skin of their teeth on earth, might slip into heaven the same way. It seemed unfair; it seemed to mock his sense of justice, but that possibility was the very essence of his religion: the parable of the laborers, the prodigal son . . . In any case, the word for what Billy Murkin was now was dead.

"Who did it, Captain Keegan?"

"That's what we're working on. A shell was found on the ramp leading to the Interstate. Have you any idea?"

"Captain, he was like a stranger to me."

"Have you ever heard the name James Dunbar?"

"James Dunbar?" Marie was clearly surprised by the irrelevancy of the question.

"Marie, we have reason to believe that Billy never left

Fox River. He has been living here for twelve years that we know of. He used the name James Dunbar."

"Here! In Fox River?"

"Yes."

"I don't believe it. I would have seen him. Someone would have seen him."

"How many people in this town knew him as Billy Murkin?"

Her altering expression told him that she no longer found Billy's return under another name an impossible feat. The only one he had to fear was Marie herself, probably, and in her mind he was thousands and thousands of miles from Fox River.

"Did you tell her where he lived?" Dowling asked when Keegan recounted the interview.

"No."

"Is there a Mrs. Dunbar, Phil?"

"Not anymore."

"Dead?"

"Yes. Just a month ago."

"So Marie has the task of burying Billy."

"There's no one else."

Circles from Keegan's solemnly dropped remark moved outward in the ensuing silence.

7

WHEN William Murkin, alias James Dunbar, first came to Fox River with his wife Marie, he had driven a delivery truck for Fobes Department Store. The job did not pay well and there was no future in it: he did the first day what he would do on the last, even if that were twenty-five years in the future. No one at Fobes remembered him for sure; the oldest person in shipping was a man with only ten years seniority, but in personnel they had a file, even a photograph that seemed to have been taken for a chauffeur's license, and one sprightly lady who was reluctant to admit that she did not remember Billy. But there was really no flesh and blood testimony to his having worked there. He had given no notice when he left, and there was no one who could say what inconvenience this might have caused, if any.

It fell to Cyril Horvath, Keegan's deputy, to do more

digging into the year Billy Murkin had driven a delivery truck for Fobes Department Store.

The woman in personnel who thought she remembered Billy had, in the interim, pored over the old files of the time, driven apparently by nothing more compelling than nostalgia. She was full of her subject when Horvath, having phoned ahead first, arrived.

"I've been wracking my brains, Lieutenant," Helen Brush said. She was a fat woman with what used to be called a Shirley Temple face. Her arms angled out from her body and she had shoes with very high heels and very pointed toes. Horvath did not care for the way she giggled when she led him into the seclusion of the room where old files were stored.

The walls were lined with boxes, there was a table with a bare bulb hanging over it. On the table were several open file folders and a thermos bottle.

"I had my lunch here," Helen Brush said. Again the giggle.

"Pretty stuffy in here, isn't it?" The room had no windows.

"Do you know, I didn't even notice. Would you like some coffee?"

"Thanks."

She had trouble getting the top off her thermos and handed it to Horvath. He twirled it off and she made a little exclamation. He half believed she would ask to feel his muscle. She poured coffee into a plastic cup, studied it, then passed it to him.

"I drank from this side," she said.

The coffee, heavily laced with milk and sugar, was only lukewarm. Which was more than could be said for this airless room.

"What I'm interested in, Mrs. Brush . . ."

"*Miss* Brush."

"I'm sorry."

"How do you think I feel?" She giggled, then grew solemn. "I just hate this Ms. business, don't you? Honestly, a girl should make it plain whether she is single or married, don't you think so?"

"Miss Brush, what I'd like to have are names of people who would have worked with Billy Murkin during his time at Fobes. Other drivers, for example."

"But they'd be retired or working somewhere else." She leaned toward him and he caught a whiff of lilac perfume. "People have a way of leaving Fobes," she whispered.

"If I had their names, I could look them up. They may be able to recall something about Billy that would be useful to us."

"You don't suppose one of them shot him, do you?"

"No. We try not to think anything like.that until we have reason to."

"He was shot?"

"That's right."

"I read about it in the paper." She shivered and tried unsuccessfully to get her fat arms around herself.

"Do you think you could do that, Miss Brush? Give me the names of the men who drove delivery trucks the year Billy Murkin was here?"

"Of course."

"And the dispatcher too."

"Gene Crawley!"

"Is he still here?"

"No. Thank God. He is an absolutely shameless old man. A man his age and he was pinching girls until the day they retired him."

"When was that?"

"Every chance he got."

"I mean, when did he retire?"

"Two years ago. And not a minute too soon." She dipped toward him, more lilac scent, a throaty giggle. "I was black and blue. We all were."

"Any trouble like that with Billy Murkin?"

"Oh, Gene stuck to girls. I don't think he bothered the men at all."

"Good. How do you spell Crawley?"

"We called him Creepy."

Horvath would have bet on it. Miss Brush was certain Gene Crawley still lived in Fox River. In fact, she had the address of the retirement home right there in her purse.

"I try to drop out and see him from time to time."

"Have you seen him recently?"

"Last Sunday. I try to cheer him up. You and I will be in a place like that someday, Lieutenant. If we're lucky. Think of that."

Horvath thought of it all the way out to Wildflower Manor, which, despite the name, had until a few years before been the county home. In a time when nearly everyone had social security, there was not much need for a county home in the traditional sense, but the fees at Wildflower Manor were kept low and there was a limit to the amount of income its occupants could have. If Gene Crawley had retired there, he could not have received much of a pension from Fobes. Any halfway decent retirement plan, together with social security, should have priced a person out of Wildflower Manor's range.

It was a red brick building in good repair; the stones lining the driveway were painted white and looked like frozen clumps of snow on the overcast March day. The snow that had fallen several days before had melted and the world had an indecisive look, neither winter nor spring. One old man in an overcoat and striped trainman's cap was huddled on a porch swing. He did not look at Horvath but continued to rock back and forth, back and forth, as if he were the pendulum measuring the passage of time in this place.

Inside, despite redecoration and the determined cheeriness of the staff, the smell of poverty still clung to the building. Crawley had a private room, on the first floor, and Horvath moved along the carpeted corridor to it. A private room, a corner room. Crawley must be one of the aristocrats of the place.

A thin reedy voice answered his knock and Horvath pushed the door open.

A very small man, wearing a bathrobe, his sparse white hair sticking straight out from his narrow skull, was rolling his legs off the bed. He stared at Horvath.

"Time for my massage?"

Horvath told him who he was. Crawley listened with a skeptical grin, lifting his hands slowly in surrender.

"I confess. I did it."

"You gonna come quietly?" After Miss Brush, Horvath was in a joking mood.

Crawley took something from the pocket of his robe and handed it to Horvath. "There it is."

"What is it?"

"Her battery."

"Whose battery?"

"Who the hell are you anyway?"

Horvath told Crawley again who he was. "I wanted to talk to you about Fobes."

Crawley displayed both palms, as if pushing Horvath away. "No, not that sweatshop." He dropped his hands. "Somebody shoot the old bastard?"

"You mean Mr. Fobes?"

"Who did it?"

"Nobody shot Mr. Fobes, Crawley. I want to know if you remember a man who used to drive a truck for Fobes. A man named Billy Murkin."

"I remember him." Crawley hadn't even hesitated.

"Are you sure?"

Crawley tapped his head. "I have a phenomenal memory. Ask anyone. Sure I remember Billy Murkin. Worked for us one year a long time ago. Ten, no, fifteen years ago."

"That's the man."

"He didn't shoot Fobes, did he?"

"Somebody shot *him,* Crawley. We're trying to figure out why."

"And you're going back fifteen years?"

"And all the years in between."

"I see. About that battery. It belongs to Margie Clapp. That's her married name." Crawley laughed piercingly. "Clapp is her married name," he cried, slapping his boney knee.

"From her hearing aid?"

Crawley got his breath. "Without that battery I can sit there and tell her anything and she smiles like an angel."

"I'll return it to her."

"Say you found it."

"Tell me about Billy Murkin."

"He wasn't fired. He should have been, but he wasn't. Thing is, any woman who let him in her house when he brought a package, well, he figured she was asking for it. He was right often enough to be excused. Of course there were complaints. They came to me. I got so many I couldn't ignore them. So I spoke to Billy about it."

"Is this the man we're discussing?"

Crawley glanced at the photograph that had been in Billy Murkin's file at Fobes. He nodded. "That's Billy."

"Did he quit after you talked to him?"

"Oh no. He stayed on another six months. As far as I could tell he was being good as gold. And then one day he quit. No notice. He just left."

"Did you ever see him again?"

"I thought he was dead."

"Why would you think that?"

Crawley squinted at Horvath. "You get my age, it seems everyone's dead. And now he is, eh? Who shot him?"

"We don't know yet."

"It wasn't me."

Horvath closed the door on the merry, mocking laughter. Crawley could afford to joke about one more death, he had seen so many. Meanwhile, he could put off thoughts of his own by whispering obscenities into Mrs. Clapp's unheeding ear and pinching the visiting Miss Brush until she was black and blue.

8

McGinnis, his white hair looking as always as if it had just been pulled from the top of an aspirin bottle, regarded Father Dowling dejectedly. The police had released the body of Billy Murkin to the McGinnis Funeral Home and Roger Dowling had come on Marie Murkin's behalf to make arrangements.

"No wake at all, Father?"

"No." Dowling decided against giving McGinnis an explanation.

"There were no children?"

The question surprised Dowling. "Why do you ask?"

"It's so sad when a widower dies. Or a widow. When there are no children. But surely he had friends. There was a respectable showing for Mrs. Dunbar."

"She was buried from here?"

McGinnis clamped a hand over his mouth and his face went pink. His eyes studied Dowling over his pudgy hand

"What is it?"

"The responsibility was his, Father. I told him it was most irregular."

"You told Mr. Dunbar?"

"No, no. The priest. Father Chirichi."

Father Dowling leaned back in his chair. "Maybe you'd better tell me all about it."

"Who told you?"

"It doesn't matter." There seemed no reason to in crease McGinnis's distress by telling him he was the only source of Dowling's information. And the funeral director was not yet a very informative source.

"You know what a stickler I am for propriety, Father. Particularly where the church is concerned. A man's parish is his, well, kingdom. I understand that. I accept that. We just can't have scavengers raiding another man's territory. Not that I put it just that way to Father Chirichi. Do you know him?"

Father Dowling certainly knew of him. Chirichi was in his early thirties, a huge man, wild-haired, given to corduroy and sweaters and ceramic crosses dangling on rawhide from his neck. A cheerful antinomian who improvised constantly in matters of dogma, liturgy, and canon law. Chirichi was particularly resistant to the idea that mankind might be divisible, even at some future date, into sheep and goats. Men were just one great big happy family, as far as Chirichi was concerned. And who were priests, mortal like other men, to say what is right and what is wrong, in any absolute sense, that is? There were rumors that Chirichi had presided at homosexual marriages. He was said to have offered Mass in the most improbable places and at equally improbable times. It was hard to say what exactly his assignment was, or that he had one at all. He had been in various Chicago parishes, but no more. The Church, he decided, should go to the people. And so, in a van, he wheeled around the diocese, alighting here and there, busy about his Father's business which his critics suspected might be the business of father Lucifer. For the past several months, Chirichi had been reported in the Fox River valley, but this was the first indication Roger Dowling had had that the young free lance had actually been in town. They had never met.

"Father Chirichi conducted Mrs. Dunbar's funeral?"

"It was only a civil ceremony. At least that's what he said when I told him that my business was within the confines of Saint Hilary's parish and that you are the pastor."

"A civil ceremony."

"He said a few prayers, of a sort, and he was very insistent to Mr. Dunbar that his wife was in heaven. He didn't want him worrying about her."

Dowling was glad that Chirichi still found the concept of heaven useful, though he doubted he would want to know the young man's definition of the term. He did not like the idea of Chirichi invading his parish, but he hoped his pique was not merely possessive. "How on earth did he know the Dunbars, Mr. McGinnis?"

"He didn't. I gather Mr. Dunbar contacted him."

"She wasn't a member of the parish."

"He insisted she was Catholic."

"Chirichi?"

"No, the husband. Father Dowling, tell me you won't hold this against me. You know my record. It was simply impossible to say no to Father Chirichi. He is a very persuasive young man. I should have known it could not remain a secret."

"I don't hold it against you. I'm not clear what exactly happened."

"The body was cremated."

Dowling nodded. That prohibition had been lifted, as

McGinnis knew. Apparently the little mortician retained a sense of guilt about it. Perhaps he still thought meat on Friday faintly illicit too. Dowling got the exchange back to the body of Marie Murkin's husband.

"James Dunbar," McGinnis said. The pink point of his tongue emerged as he wrote.

"William Murkin," Dowling corrected.

"I beg your pardon."

"That is his true name. Weren't you told?"

"Murkin? But your housekeeper . . ."

Dowling nodded. McGinnis could be forgiven for not knowing that the corpse had two names. The *Fox River Messenger*'s story had been vague, whether out of mercy or out of Mervel's benign neglect of facts it would be difficult to say. Ninian's story for the *Tribune* was both shorter and more informative. Would the subscribers of one paper pass on to the subscribers of the other the news that Marie Murkin's husband had been living with another woman mere miles from the rectory? Well, McGinnis had to be told. The mortician hitched his chair forward and folded his little hands on his desk top. His expression was avid. Secrets. Roger Dowling stifled the urge to look with contempt on McGinnis's curiosity. Which of us does not have an insatiable appetite for information about other people?

9

Mrs. Herman Hanson's bridge group, three tables, met on Thursday afternoons and it seemed providential that today the girls should be coming to her. God knows that each of them had dropped by during the short time Marie Murkin was in her house and several of them in the aftermath of her stay but there were so many facets of the scandalous situation still undiscussed that it promised a lively afternoon. Even so, dedicated as they were, they played two rubbers before Harriet Siska was dummy at the same time as Flo Hanson and the subject was finally raised.

"How could the poor woman return to the rectory, Flo? I understand she's sleeping in the very room in which her husband was killed."

"He was her husband, wasn't he, Flo? I mean, that's true?"

"Father Dowling never indicated otherwise."

"I've never heard of a murder in a rectory before."

"My husband said there was some very crude speculation about it at his office. Priest, housekeeper, murdered husband. You can imagine."

"They don't know Father Dowling."

That was when the conversation took a turn away from Marie Murkin's husband and never really got back to him. Bunny Flynn, a new member of the group, new to Fox River, recently moved here from some town in Wisconsin whose name Flo could not remember, a long Indian name, Bunny wanted to know what the others really thought of Father Dowling.

"As a pastor, I mean. In the new Church."

Bunny was assured that St. Hilary's had been built in the forties. Flo saw the girl wince. "I meant the postconciliar church. Dick and I couldn't believe it when we attended our first liturgy at Saint Hilary's."

Bunny meant the Mass and she went on to explain that, in Wisconsin, the parish had been organized around a pastoral team, that the laity participated in the running of the parish, and not only financially.

"Not only! What else do they do?"

It seemed that in Wisconsin lay people taught the religion classes, they had discussion groups that met in one another's homes, that at the eucharistic assembly—Bunny meant the Mass—lay people were readers during the liturgy of the word, women too. She made it sound very exciting. Certainly Bunny was excited.

"But what really floored me is the way my Judy is being prepared for confirmation."

There were to be confirmations at St. Hilary's in scarcely more than a week and several of the bridge players had children in the small class of *confirmandi*—the word was Bunny's. Her Judy had been abject when she found that nothing was the way it had been in Wisconsin when her brother Matt was confirmed. Bunny and Dick, the whole family, really, had been involved, and the kids had made banners and coats of arms and there had been lots of meetings with filmstrips and brainstorming and all kinds of things.

"On the day itself, well, you could just feel the Holy Spirit sweeping through the parish."

Nobody knew quite what to say to that. Finally Flo asked Bunny if she had spoken to Father Dowling about this.

Bunny looked puzzled. "That's why I wanted to know what you girls think of him. He seemed very curious about what I had to say, he asked a lot of questions, and I felt very good about the visit until a day later when it dawned on me that however nice he had been he hadn't said a thing about doing things differently at Saint Hilary's."

"He teaches the confirmation class himself."

"I know! And he uses a catechism." Bunny's eyes rounded in shock.

"Well, the kids have to know what they're about to do."

"But do they? It's just questions and answers. Has he ever asked them if they really want to be confirmed?"

"If they want to?"

"Yes! After all, it's the sacrament of maturity. They're supposed to be becoming adults in the faith. Well, you ask adults if they want to do something; you don't just tell them."

"But what if some kid says he doesn't want to?"

"My Matthew refused the first time," Bunny said triumphantly. "When he was confirmed, finally, it was his decision."

Flo looked around at the bright smiles on the faces of her friends as they listened to Bunny, but she was not deceived. They all loved Father Dowling, now that they were used to him. Unlike his predecessor, Monsignor Hunniker, he never mentioned money. And he was, they agreed, a saintly man. It was a comfort to know that he was among them, doing what a priest should do, praying for them.

"Whose deal?" Harriet Siska demanded and almost immediately there was silence again save for the slap of cards on the tables. Flo was relieved, but she was a little miffed too. She had expected to go into great detail on Marie Murkin's stay with her. She had the narrative down to perfection now and while she had not rehearsed it, exactly, she had been looking forward to enthralling her guests with the definitive version. Darn Bunny Flynn anyway.

10

DURING her many years as housekeeper of the St. Hilary's rectory, Marie Murkin had adopted an attitude toward those who came seeking solace and guidance from the priests, an attitude she had supposed to be, when she thought of it at all,

clerical, official, professional. Give me your tired, your poor
. . . She smiled wryly. Is that what she had seemed, a presumptuous Statue of Liberty when she opened the door? Welcome to Ellis Island, you wretches. Her own painful past had somehow been swept away before the tide of woe that flowed into the rectory. Not that she was privy to whatever brought people here, except in those not infrequent cases of people who just started to talk as soon as she opened the door. Perhaps they justified the manner she had developed over the years. And yet, how ironic it seemed to her now.

Who was more beaten and broken than she? Oh, all you who pass by the way, see if there is any sorrow like unto my sorrow. Mrs. Murkin was in the crowded church where Father Dowling led the congregation in the stations of the cross. Tears came to her eyes as he recited the familiar words, put into the mouth of Mary. She was glad that Father Dowling had made the stations part of the Parish Lenten observance again. Kneeling in a back pew, crushed in anonymously with the others, no longer feeling she was different from the rest of the congregation, somebody special, the housekeeper of the rectory, she thought that the words attributed to our Blessed Mother had application to herself as well.

It angered her to recognize that it was her own embarrassment rather than Billy's death that cut most deeply. Why had he come back to her after all those years? She had thought of him as being impossibly far off, and now she knew he had been living scarcely a stone's throw away. It seemed incredible that they could live in the same city and never run into each other, but of course her life was confined to her work. She went downtown by cab on Mondays to put the collection in the bank and did what little shopping she did then. For the most part, she was in the rectory, in her kitchen or upstairs in her room. Sometimes she had thought of her life as being otherworldly, almost a nun's life, but she had a color TV in her room and when she was up there it was on. She never watched during the day, however, and that was a cross of sorts. Her life was comfortable. Father Dowling was certainly easy enough to cook for; there seemed nothing he didn't like and he always said how well prepared the food was. Really, she lived in a cocoon. And then, out of the blue, out of the snow, Billy had walked in, just walked in and a few hours later he was dead, shot, lying across her bed, his head a bloody mess.

Marie raised her hand to her face and pressed her balled-up handkerchief to her mouth. In the main aisle of the church, Father Dowling moved along, stopping at each station, genuflecting, intoning, and then they all responded. She tried to concentrate on what he was saying. She was here to pray, not to feel sorry for herself. She was reminded of the pathetic funeral they had given Billy. A Mass to which not many even of the curious came, since there had been no announcement of it, and then at the cemetery just Father Dowling, Marie, her brother Bob, McGinnis and his men.

She had wept, but it had been as much for herself as for Billy. Billy had been a stranger when he stepped into the rectory kitchen. He had been living with another woman, living in sin, in violation of church law and of state law too. A bigamist. Had the other woman known? She could not have. What is more ridiculous than to be a wife of a bigamist? It turned one's life into a joke, a very bad joke. Billy's sense of humor had been his least appealing trait. But that other woman, dead now too, seemed mythical and unreal. Marie could not feel resentment toward her. The fact was that, finally, Billy had come back to her, to Marie. She would never know what his intentions had been, but the fact that he had indeed come back was a kind of apology. Father Dowling had once said that if someone enters the confessional the assumption that he was contrite must be made. Honestly, when she thought of the conversations she had had with pastors over the years. They did talk to her as if she knew all about it, was almost a priest herself, someone who would understand. Shop talk.

After the stations there was benediction of the Blessed Sacrament and then the service was over and the congregation went out into the chilly night. Marie knelt on, watching the altar boys extinguish the candles. Scattered through the church were a few stragglers, the devout, perhaps just the lonely. Captain Keegan rose, genuflected and came down the side aisle. Their eyes met and he stopped to speak to her.

"Could I have a word with you, Mrs. Murkin?"

She got up, bobbed, crossed herself and followed Captain Keegan into the vestibule.

"We don't seem to be making much progress, I'm sorry to say."

"I've been thinking."

"Yes?" Keegan was alert, as if he thought she had done what he had urged her to do: think of something significant Billy had said. But what?

"Captain, maybe it was just an accident. I mean, an accident that it was Billy. You read of these crazy people who just start shooting. They don't care who they're shooting at."

"There was only the one shot, Mrs. Murkin."

"Maybe whoever did it wasn't even aiming at anyone. Maybe he didn't even intend to shoot. Maybe he doesn't know to this day that he actually killed someone."

Keegan nodded, but she could see that such maybes did not really interest him. He had to assume that things happened because someone meant them to happen But that kind of thinking was not getting him anywhere, by his own admission. Marie could almost imagine some boy out with his rifle, taking aim, pulling the trigger, bang, bang. Just a game. The way it had been when she and her brother Bob were young. If the boy had seen Billy, a man in a window a great distance off, he would not have seemed a real live human being. Of course it was awful to think that some child had done it and was walking around now carrying his dreadful secret. Marie preferred to think that he did not even know he had hit someone.

"Are you coming to the rectory, Captain?"

"Does Father Dowling expect me?"

"I don't know."

Keegan was disappointed. What a lonely life he must lead.

"You know you're always welcome."

"Not tonight, Marie. I'll be stopping by the office on my way home."

He pulled up the collar of his topcoat and squinted into the night. A very light snow was falling, the flakes silvery against the outside lights. The thought of her snug little room and her color TV beckoned to Marie.

Keegan had gone on and Marie, fussing with her gloves, saw the girl who had come twice to see Father Dowling. She was dipping her fingers into the holy water font. She blessed herself with great concentration, as if she had just learned how. A strange girl. Marie was sorry that Father Dowling had never hinted at the purpose of the visits. It might have been marriage, but the girl always came alone. Eunice Flanagan.

Remembering the name brought a smile to Marie's lips. She did not like to forget a name. She was smiling when the girl glanced at her. A timid smile at Marie and then swiftly into the night. A good idea. Back to the rectory.

Outside the snowy night was like the one out of which Billy Murkin had come back to her. Marie shivered as if he were still about and might come again and knock on the kitchen door. More likely it would be her brother Bob.

11

Eunice Flanagan did not like being recognized by the parish housekeeper when she left St. Hilary's church after stations of the cross.

That had to be the woman she had read about in the paper, the one whose husband had returned after fifteen years only to be shot dead within hours of their reunion. Eunice imagined that the husband had been some sort of underworld figure and she found it a strange thought that a gangster's wife should be cooking for Father Dowling.

Eunice's economy car was freezing cold and the plastic seat crackled and complained when she slid behind the wheel. The motor started right away but there was no reason to hope that the heater would provide any heat. The windows had a way of frosting over, steaming with her breath, even when she was alone in the car. It had a manual shift, she got thirty miles to the gallon and that was the point of the car, but Eunice liked nothing better than to get behind the wheel of one of her father's cars. Real cars. Plush and comfortable and warm. And quiet. Driving her own car was reminiscent of directing a tractor mower across the family lawn.

Images of home. She had moved back to her parents' house and her mother, instead of being happy, had turned it into an occasion for worry.

"Is anything wrong, Eunice?"

She puttered about the kitchen, at the stove, at a cupboard, putting things before her daughter. Eunice was convinced that her mother would die in motion, frozen like some figure on a vase.

"It just seemed a waste of money. The apartment."

"Have you been running up bills?"

"No."

"Is it that boy again?"

Boy. Eunice just stared at her mother. If Andy Pilsen was her idea of a boy, when did people count as grownup?

"Has he been bothering you again, Eunice?"

That was the question she should have put to her mother. How awful it had been to learn that Andy had actually shown up at the house, demanding to speak to her parents. Her father had not been there at the time and her mother had no idea what Andy was talking about. It had come as news to her that she and her husband were opposing Eunice's marriage, though Andy's appearance had obviously encouraged the idea. Her father, relying on her mother's description of the visit, had raged and fumed and wished to God he had been home when that maniac burst into his house demanding they turn over their daughter to him. Of course they had wanted to know how well she knew Andy and she had said, well, yes, she knew him, they had met, but marriage?

Her voice had risen out of control, refusing to become the incredulous laugh she intended. Later she got Andy s version

"If you ever do that again," she told him, "I'll never speak to you again."

"If you ever do that again, I'll never speak to you again." He mimicked her words, flouncing about his room as he did so. She wished he would put on some clothes No one can be taken seriously when they are not wearing clothes "You sound just like her, do you know that? No wonder you're a psychological mess."

"Thanks."

"I mean it. You're a classical case. Admit it, you think you're betraying your parents when you go to bed with me."

She did not answer, but it was true. She was betraying her parents, her principles, herself. Maybe she was sick, going to bed with a man she found repulsive. Maybe she had counted on her parents, particularly her mother, to find Andy impossible. Certainly she had had no sense of telling a lie when she informed Andy that her parents would not let her marry him.

"Not *let* you! You're a big girl, Eunice. You can do anything you want. You're independent."

Independent like him? Without help from her parents, she could never have afforded the apartment in which she had briefly lived. The apartment she did not need. It was a pretense of independence that needed a subsidy from her father to be kept up. Majoring in history is not a proximate preparation for the real world. The job Eunice had, receptionist for the law firm of Morrissey and Morrissey, was one she could have handled out of high school. Out of grade school, for that matter. All she did was answer the phone, smile, usher clients to the appropriate office, occasionally type. And the pay was awful. Morrissey and Morrissey was one of the most prosperous firms in Fox River but it was clear that they had no intention of sharing the wealth, not even with the daughter of one of their more important clients. Flanagan Construction, once Flanagan Sheet Metal, required the full-time attention of one junior partner, two law clerks, and the frequent attention of the elder Mr. Morrissey. If Eunice had tried to live on her salary alone, she would be living in squalor, like Andy Pilsen.

Even her apartment had seemed like slumming to her, but giving it up and going back to her parents' home had been motivated as much by the dread of Andy visiting her there as by the apartment's inadequacies. As far as he knew, she had always lived at home.

The fact that her mother asked if Andy was bothering her again indicated that they accepted her story that he was just some pest she hardly knew. Now, this Friday night, having attended the stations of the cross at St. Hilary's, having half seriously asked God's forgiveness for lying about Andy to both her parents and to Father Dowling, Eunice drove toward the bar where Andy worked. The streets were wet with snow and her tires made a hissing sound as she drove. It had been a week since she had seen Andy, though they had talked on the phone several times. She had given him the number of Morrissey and Morrissey and he called her in the morning when he got up, which was when she was having lunch. She ate at her desk, almost everybody else was out of the office, so it was possible for them to talk. And she could always break off by claiming that a business call was coming in. She would put Andy on Hold and leave him there, sometimes for five minutes, and that made him mad as the dickens.

"Andy, I have a job. My job is to answer the phone. You know that."

"For five minutes?"

"This is a very busy office."

"Don't tell me how busy the office is.

"Okay."

"Okay what?"

"Okay I won't tell you how busy the office is."

Then he had hung up on her. Turn about is fair play.

Eunice smiled through the steamy windshield of her little car, smiled but did not feel in the least bit happy. In church, joining with the others, reminded of chapel when she was at college, she had suddenly felt a complete stranger to herself. It was as though she had created another self to do things with Andy, a self she did not like at all. Her other self, her real self, was there in the church, addressing God, accepting His law and love and wanting to be what He meant her to be. Sometimes she recalled the dream she had had as a girl, a dream of becoming a nun and giving her life for others, with no thought of herself. Like Mother Teresa in Calcutta. A saint.

At college one of the older nuns had urged her to read a novel of Léon Bloy's. *The Woman Who Was Poor*. It was a powerful book, a frightening book, but its theme was summed up in a single line. There is only one tragedy, not to be a saint. That line could still affect Eunice in the most powerful way. If it was indeed true, then her life was tragic, most lives were. She squinted her eyes and heard as if from a distance the voice of Father Dowling and the answering voices of the congregation and they might have been voices of saints, separate from herself, in an elsewhere of peace and joy, while she lived a life of lies and discontent, sleeping with Andy Pilsen. How easy it was to hate the innocent.

The bar had the ridiculous name, The Mangy Manger. At this hour it was like a vision of hell. Dimly lit, the noise of the band ear-splitting, smoke-filled, no one speaking in a normal voice, and, on the diminutive dance floor, people writhing in time to the bestial beat of that dreadful music Eyes closed, pale, their expressions those of the doomed and damned—what an utterly joyless place it was. Eunice told herself that it was in the nature of a Lenten penance to come here.

From behind the bar, Andy caught her eye. He indicated a kind of opening before him, but she had to wedge herself between bodies that refused to give way for her. Andy already had a stinger ready for her. He was speaking. She had to read his lips. The din was enormous and getting worse; the bar area seemed to get the brunt of it. No wonder Andy complained of headaches. He was telling her he would take a break as soon as he could.

An elbow in her side, a buttock pressed against her hip, arms reaching across and past her. Eunice shuddered at this sweaty impersonal contact. An orgy must be like this. An orgy of the kind Andy read to her about from the porno-graphic paperbacks he had in his room. That had been an-other assault on her prudishness, but she had preferred the novels to the magazines whose photographs made her want to throw up. Hell is all around us; we are damning ourselves with our deeds. How could a soul drenched in such filth and corruption bear to see God? It would have made itself unfit for that vision, but to go on without God is hell. These things were so much easier to believe now that she knew what they referred to.

"Where you been?"

They stood in the lesser din by the door that gave onto the side parking lot. In the light of the spot whose beam cut through the smoke-filled air to guide newcomers into the deeper gloom, Andy looked pale and vexed.

'Church.

"What?"

"I've been to church." She had to shout and she felt absurd when a passing couple turned to stare at her. It was better to simply mouth words. Andy had become adept at reading lips as a result of working here and he glowered at her.

"Where?"

"Guess." She knew what his guess would be. He hated Father Dowling without knowing him. Hatred came with difficulty after one had met the priest.

"Were you saved?"

"Not yet." In an antic mood, she added, "I prayed for you.'

"Don't bother."

"It's easy."

He shook his head violently. "I wish you'd lay off that stuff. You don't fool me."

He put his arm around her waist and drew her tight against him, the deed meant to remind her of her supposed abandon in his bed. How clinical those sessions were, how joyless. The prospect of perpetual chastity seemed impossibly attractive after their grotesqueries.

"Just myself."

"What?" He shouted in her ear.

"I only fool myself."

He could not understand. It was stupid trying to converse here. A metaphor of alienation. She mouthed the phrase. It was the sort of jargon Andy loved, with his piecemeal education and vast pretensions to intellectual sophistication. But he could not read her lips. She had been in shadow and now she moved her face into the light.

"I confess," she said.

His eyes were suddenly full of fury and his arm was

painful about her. He was hissing something in her ear, but that was all she heard, a hiss. He might have been a reptile, a snake, Satan himself. She realized he had misunderstood. He thought that she had gone to confession. How ludicrous he was, a nineteenth-century figure, someone out of Huysmans, hating the priests and their doings, their presumed control over the simple faithful.

When he asked if she would wait until his shift was over, she agreed.

She would go with him to his room.

She had told her mother that she was spending the night in Chicago. With a friend. Did she have any friends? Sometimes it seemed that all she had was Andy.

12

BUNNY FLYNN was nice as pie. She sat on the edge of the chair, her purse on her lap, a smile on her lips. Whenever Father Dowling spoke, she nodded as if to encourage him or to reassure him that he was not really interrupting.

"What was the name of your parish in Wisconsin?"

"In Whichawa? Precious Blood." She winced. "But it was a very progressive parish."

"Ah."

"The pastoral team was made up of Brendanites."

"Brendanites?"

"Society of Saint Brendan. It's a small order."

"But progressive?"

"I can't speak for all of them, but the men at Precious Blood were truly men of Vatican Two."

"I hope we are all that."

He seemed to have given Mrs. Flynn an opening. "I'm so glad to hear you say that, Father Dowling. The thing we missed most when we got here, Dick and I, were parish committees."

"Oh, we have lots of groups. The Rosary Society. The Altar Society."

Her smile was beatific. "I meant administrative committees."

"For example?"

"Liturgical. Educational. Financial. Spiritual."

"What exactly does a spiritual committee do?"

"Neither of us was on that one. I gather they prayed a lot." A frown nettled her brow. "I think they got pretty charismatic."

Father Dowling's smile seemed to have a life of its own, as if his must match Mrs. Flynn's. She was, he was certain, a devout and zealous woman. Why then did he see her as a threat to the pastoral idyll life at St. Hilary's had been since he came here? Was she the wave of the future or simply a passing annoyance? It was difficult to say. He wanted to be receptive. He did not want, in what he was woefully certain would be her phrase, to turn her off. But neither did he want to encourage her.

"We also had a sick committee. To visit hospitals and to take the eucharist to the bedridden."

"Lay people did that?"

"Of course."

"How many Brendanites were on the pastoral team in . . . " He groped for the name of the town in Wisconsin where the future was the present.

"Whichawa. There were three priests and a brother."

"It must have been a huge parish."

"No bigger than Saint Hilary's."

Father Dowling was puzzled. "Then why didn't the priests take communion to the sick?"

Her expression made him feel retarded. "Aren't we all priests, in a way?"

"I suppose each of us is everything, in a way. And anything."

"You don't approve of lay participation?"

His hesitation apparently spoke volumes to Bunny Flynn. Lay participation was such a commodious phrase that Father Dowling did not know how to be for it or against it. He sensed that they were in choppy waters and he really did not want to exchange opinions on the nature of the priesthood and the lay estate with Bunny Flynn. He hoped that he himself had no opinions on such matters. It was not what went down in Whichawa, a random consensus reached here or there, that defined these things. He knew that there were priests—and it was impossible to suppress the thought of the ineffable Chirichi—who professed themselves ignorant of what a priest is. Well, there was no confusion in the Church's teaching on the subject, least of all in the documents of Vatican II.

"You said you wanted to talk about the confirmation class."

"Yes. Not that it isn't connected with these other things. I thought I might share with you the way confirmation was administered in Whichawa."

As parody, the account she gave of the liturgical

shenanigans of her erstwhile parish might have held some
interest, but there was little doubt that Bunny Flynn thought
Father Dowling might profit from the telling, perhaps decide
to incorporate some of its bolder elements into the coming
celebration at St. Hilary's.

"I'll certainly talk to the bishop about it," he
promised.

"Oh, would you, Father? We would really appreciate
that."

"We?"

"Dick and I."

He hoped that meant she had not been stirring up
discontent in the parish. How many would be susceptible to
the appeal of these witless innovations? Not many, he prayed.
He resolved to make it a special intention of his prayers from
now on. It had not occurred to him that St. Hilary's was a
redoubt of sanity and taste. Reverence and decorum should be
the watchwords of worship so far as Father Dowling was concerned. Bunny Flynn had taken a folded sheet from her purse
and now handed it to him.

"I happened to have a copy of this. It might give you
some ideas."

"Thank you."

She got to her feet when he did. He accompanied her
to the front door where she hesitated. "What is your first
name?"

"Roger."

"I wish you'd call me Bunny." She stepped outside.
"Good-by, Roger. And thanks."

The sheet, when he unfolded it, proved to be mimeo-
graphed, stanzas of a hymn, no music. A note indicated that
the tune of *Shenandoah* should be used. The text was copy-
righted, taken from a hymnal published in Missouri whose

• 66 •

title was *Hi God!* Father Dowling took the sheet with him to his office where he dropped it into the wastebasket.

The celebrant at the confirmation ceremony would be Bishop Arthur Rooney, one-time colleague of Roger Dowling on the marriage tribunal and earlier a classmate both at the seminary and at Catholic University in Washington where they had earned their doctorates in canon law. The similarity between the two men continued into the physical order: same height, same thin frames, same sharp profiles. Their joint reports had been known as by-Gemini documents. Their priestly paths might have been identical too, since it was from such vineyards as the marriage tribunal that bishops were selected, as indeed Art Rooney had been selected. It would not be fair to say that Rooney had been a better bureaucrat than Dowling, but he certainly showed less wear and tear from the sad tasks that had befallen them. The marriage court did not, because it could not, encourage hope in those who brought their cases to it, petitioning annulments, but of course the very fact that a case was accepted and that many people were devoting hours to its study stirred up hope, a hope that in the vast majority of cases was ultimately dashed. The emphasis had to be on *ultimately,* since the tribunal, in its efforts to be fair and thorough, spent years on cases, years during which hope was strained, embittered, died. Often new marriages were entered into by the impatient, thus complicating the work of the tribunal.

Roger Dowling had anguished with the claimants, had aged with the cases, had fallen into the trap of drink to escape the burden of his duties. Rooney had done none of these things, certainly not the last. He found the law a more reward ing mistress than Dowling did. No one was surprised when Arthur Rooney was named an auxiliary bishop. For some years now Bishop Rooney's life had been one of assisting the cardinal, making parish visitations, conferring confirmation. Dowling was sure that Rooney performed these tasks with every bit as much zeal and punctiliousness as he had his previous ones.

When Father Dowling dialed the chancery and asked for Bishop Rooney he was put through to a secretary.

"May I tell Bishop Rooney who is calling, please?"

"Roger Dowling."

She seemed to be consulting something. "The bishop is terribly busy this afternoon, Mr. Dowling."

"Father Dowling."

"Father, I'm sorry," she trilled. "One moment, please."

While he waited, Roger Dowling reflected that Bunny Flynn would not have approved of the clericalism obviously rampant among employees of the archdiocesan chancery.

"Roger?"

"Hello, Bishop. I know I don't have to remind you that you'll be confirming here at Saint Hilary's next week."

"I'm looking forward to it. I hope we'll have an opportunity for a good long talk. Can you put me up for the night?"

"Of course."

"I trust I won't be shot at."

"I wondered if you'd read about that."

"There haven't been any repercussions?"

"Oh, no. Mrs. Murkin is doing quite well."

"Ah, the housekeeper. It was her husband, was it not?"

"Her estranged husband. They hadn't seen one another for fifteen years until the day he was shot."

"Extraordinary. I don't recall hearing if they caught the one who did it."

"They're still working on it. Bishop, about the confirmation. A new parishioner was just in to tell me how they did these things in her previous parish. I hope you won't object to a very traditional ceremony."

"Roger, I'm counting on it."

"Are these innovations common? Some of the things this woman mentioned . . . "

"You wouldn't believe what I've sometimes encountered, Roger. I have never thought of myself as a conservative, as you know, but there have been times when I've felt absolutely Neanderthal. Have you heard of a society that has been formed to oppose absolutely anything that is new? That isn't the title, but it might as well be. Some place in California, of course. There are days when I would like to join. Those days usually follow confirming in some *avant-garde* place."

"Does it happen often?"

"No, but it seems to. How do you like pastoral life?"

"I love it."

And that, he reflected after he had hung up, was the simple truth of the matter. By all the usual calculations, well, by chancery calculations, he was not a successful priest. His appointment to St. Hilary's had been met by commiseration at best, with reassurance at worst. "Give it a few years, Roger," Art Rooney had said. "Show them you have what it takes. Men have been brought back from the boondocks before."

Now the thought of being called back to the kind of work he had spent most of his priestly life doing filled him with dread. It was unlikely in the extreme that this might happen, Art Rooney had only meant to be kind. Perhaps Roger Dowling had himself regarded Fox River, Illinois, as exile, some St. Helena of the clerical wars, but almost immediately upon arrival he had recognized it as the place where he belonged. It had promised obscurity, a small stage, a place to offer what remained of his broken life to God. His people were like himself, at least with regard to their liturgical predilections. He would have been loath to turn over to others the classes in Christian doctrine. The parish school no longer existed, a casualty of demographic changes; the families of the parish were predominantly middle-aged, their children grown and gone. Those who had children sent them to the public schools and they came to Roger Dowling for religious instruction. He had prepared the confirmation class himself and if there would be none of the hoopla Bunny Flynn had wanted, these young men and women were ready to accept adult status in the church, to be, in the catechism phrase, soldiers of Jesus Christ. With the class, he looked forward to the day when they would receive the Holy Ghost. Holy Spirit, he corrected In the age of the vernacular, good Anglo-Saxon words were re placed with others of more recondite origin, usually from the Greek. homily, eucharistic assembly, charism.

A copy of Dante lay on Dowling's desk. It was his favorite book after the Roman Breviary, which he continued to recite each day in the old long form in Latin. A bit of nostalgia there, perhaps, a palpable link with the young man he had been years ago in the seminary when, a year before ordination, he had accepted along with celibacy the obligation to read the daily office from the breviary, the hours made up of psalms, selections from the gospels and epistles, from the Church Fathers. And the glorious hymns. Dowling's eye strayed to the wastebasket and the abomination he had been handed by Bunny Flynn. *Hi God!* He shuddered. Such tasteless trash. The dwindling faithful were put through such agonies by trivializations of worship that sought to blur the distinction between sacred and secular.

So Dowling was relieved, if not surprised, that Bishop Rooney would not come in the expectation of a jazzy celebration, handcrafted signs, slogans and other items that had enraptured Whichawa, if Bunny Flynn was to be believed. This he permitted himself to doubt. How many, even in Whichawa, had gritted their teeth and borne the abominations, their aesthetic anguish an acceptable sacrifice?

He opened the Dante, a large volume, the Inferno illustrations by Gustave Doré Since childhood, it seemed, he had read this book and pored over these horrendous engravings which gave to the eye images Dante addressed to the very soul. *Lasciate ogni speranza* . . . But reading Dante proved an inexhaustible reservoir of hope.

His office had grown dark as he sat there; the gloaming and his conversation with Bishop Rooney reminded him of the marriage tribunal. There was some connection that was trying to establish itself in his mind. Almost dreamily, he pulled the telephone toward him, checked a number in the directory, and dialed.

"Mr. McGinnis here."

The voice was sepulchral and vaguely expectant. The note of expectancy grew when Father Dowling identified himself.

"Yes, Father. I am at your disposal."

"Just a question, Mr. McGinnis."

"Of course." But the voice modulated. Poor McGinnis. A good day for him was one on which the obituary column, that Dow-Jones of the undertaker, was long.

"The other day you showed me your records on Mrs. Dunbar."

"Is something wrong?"

"Do you have them handy?"

"Just a moment." Offstage noises and then, "Yes. I have them."

"Would you read her name?"

'Her name?"

"The complete name."

McGinnis read it, slowly, as if reciting a lesson Father Dowling thanked him.

"Is that all?"

"Yes. Thank you, Mr. McGinnis."

He put down the phone, sat back in his chair, and rubbed his eyes with the tips of his fingers. Blanche Quirk Dunbar. The maiden name, not uncommon, but striking nonetheless, had seemed to lift to meet his gaze when he glanced at the form McGinnis had shown him. Quirk. Ah. There had been a marriage involving someone with that name. Years ago. Quirk and . . . But he could not think of the other party. Doubtless it was just a coincidence.

But, like his friend Phil Keegan, Roger Dowling did not really believe in coincidence.

13

WHEN William Flanagan began what was to become Flanagan Construction, he had spent most of his day in the shop or on job sites and the weariness with which he had gone to bed at night was physical, acquired with sweat and the straining of muscles. Now he spent his day in a chair—behind a desk, at a conference table, drawn up to a lunch or dinner table. He was as sedentary as Rodin's "Thinker," and as immobile. For exercise, he did push-ups in his office with the door locked, and twice a week he worked out at the Fox River Athletic Club Sports, he realized, are the arts of the indolent, imitations of meaningful labor. He was trapped now but would not have escaped if he could. Early and late, active or sedentary, his driving motive had been to make the Flanagan enterprise flourish.

Just sitting and reading seemed to sum up his job, a mile of memos a day, running reports that enabled him to keep an eye on what the hell was going on in a business he supposedly ran. A copy of every letter ended on his desk. He read this mass of material at the office, between appointments, as a relief from more taxing problems; he took it home with him. Thus it was that, one night at eleven o'clock, seated in a leather chair in the den, a highball close at hand, he read the memo from plant security telling him the police had made inquiries about a former employee, James Dunbar. That was all. Flanagan turned the memo over, on the off chance that there was more. There was not. No follow-up at all.

At two-thirty, when his unreliable bladder drove him from his bed he found himself thinking again of the Dunbar memo. He did not like it. He did not like so uninformative a communiqué. Before he got back into bed, he made a note to call Cowper in the morning.

"That's all there was," Cowper said. Flanagan left him standing in front of him, literally on the carpet. "It was just routine."

"They just dropped by to ask about Dunbar?"

Cowper, middle-sized so far as height was concerned, glanced at the door open to the outer office. "He was shot. He's dead. That's why they came here. Routine."

"We could use a little routine of our own," Flanagan

said meaningfully. He shook the memo, let it flutter to the desk. "Get out of here."

Cowper found the gruffness reassuring. He made a little salute and got out of there.

That night Eunice read the newspaper story to him.

"I know Father Dowling," she said in wondrous tones. "That's his parish."

"I've heard of him."

"He's very old-fashioned. Very strict. You'd like him."

But Flanagan remembered that it was Morrissey who had mentioned Dowling to him, and Morrissey had been annoyed. Morrissey would like an old-fashioned priest if anyone would. Flanagan was willing to let his daughter think that he himself went around ranking priests. He did not understand Eunice at all.

If he was not going to have sons, he should have had a dozen daughters. It made no sense, a man like himself, with just one daughter From the time she was a little girl Eunice had seemed fragile and vulnerable and his guts knotted up at the thought of anything happening to her. He had never been able to show his love for her without being clumsy and thus embarrassing both Eunice and himself. He was too big, he was too gruff, he had to watch his language lest he talk at home the way he had to at the office. He had sent Eunice to convent schools and then to Rosary College and her record had been excellent. There had been a time when Zoe feared and he had hoped that Eunice was thinking of becoming a nun. William Flanagan would have been pleased with a daughter who had dedicated her life to God, in the cloister, safe. And praying for him. Eunice had once brought home a book about Thérèse of Lisieux, the Little Flower, and if Wild Bill Flanagan could not quite see himself in the role of Thérèse's father, Eunice seemed to fill the bill as a nun.

But that was not to be and it was difficult to regret it

when you saw the way nuns were running around now. So get married and have kids and make him a grandfather. Then someone else would have shouldered part of the burden of worrying about Eunice. But she had nothing serious going at all; she never had had. Zoe was not worried, she thought everything was hunky-dory, but here was a girl nearly twenty-four years old, doing a flunky's job at Morrissey and Morrissey. And going to talk to Father Dowling. About what?

"Just to talk."

Couldn't she talk to her father if she had to talk to somebody? He would like to know what the hell was going on in her head.

Eunice. Dowling. Dunbar. The newspaper account was a surprise. The man who had worked for Flanagan for a dozen years under the name Dunbar was actually Billy Murkin whose wife was a housekeeper for Father Dowling at St. Hilary's rectory.

Cowper reported the following day. He had asked around, to see what kind of man people thought Dunbar/Murkin had been. He had not come up with much. The man's life had apparently been thought quiet and regular. His wife, his second wife, had died a month before him. Cowper reported the speculation that loneliness had driven Dunbar back to his first wife.

Flanagan shrugged. The important thing was that, whatever lay behind the violent end of James Dunbar, it was not connected with Flanagan Construction. Cowper assured him about that. It was a good thing. Wild Bill Flanagan would tolerate no threat to the business he had built. He felt a fierce, protective devotion to it. Almost a tenderness. Sometimes it occurred to him that his attitude toward his company and toward his daughter was the same. Flanagan told Cowper to keep an eye on the situation.

Cowper was a retired cop. That meant that he could

shoot straight and was lazy as sin. Presumably, there was the added benefit of Cowper's contacts with his old buddies still on the force. Such contact should keep Cowper informed on where the police were in their investigation of the shooting of Dunbar/Murkin.

14

WHERE the police were in their investigation of the death of Marie Murkin's husband was nowhere. Horvath and Keegan, the reports before them, looked at one another.

Keegan said, "The only one here who had a motive for shooting him was Marie Murkin."

"How is she with a deer rifle?"

"It would have been the trick shot of the century."

It said something about the impasse they had reached that Keegan leaned back in his chair and imagined Marie Murkin slipping out of the rectory, driving to the ramp leading to the Interstate, taking a pot shot at the husband she had positioned at her bedroom window, then hurrying back to the rectory to serve dinner. Apart from the fact that Marie did not drive, had probably never shot a weapon of any kind, and could not see five hundred yards to save her life, it was a beautiful theory.

"Some kid," Horvath said.

"I'll buy that when you find him."

"He wouldn't have a motive."

"He'd have a rifle. One we could match the slug to."

"And he could live in Peoria."

Keegan frowned. He did not like it. He did not like irrational explanations. There were too many unexplained events for his taste as it was. He did not want to add to their number in his official capacity.

"Nothing at Flanagan's?"

"For a guy who worked there twelve years, he was almost a stranger. He made a bigger impression at Fobes in one year."

Horvath had written up his interview with Crawley. It was too long. That was the sort of thing you did on a case like this, embroider the non-facts. He himself had written three pages on his talk with Marie Murkin, but he could have put it on a postcard with room to spare. She had no idea who had shot her husband. He was a stranger to her. The second wife was dead, which cut off that avenue. The neighbors?

"They talked over the fence, said hello, but that was about it."

"What the hell did they do for recreation?"

"Drink."

Horvath's huge index finger pointed to a page. The Dunbars had had a whopping weekly liquor bill. A regular supply, delivered on Tuesdays, three bourbon, three Scotch, sweet and dry vermouth, a case of 3.2 beer. They gave no parties.

"What did she die of, cirrhosis?"

"Should I find out?"

"Find out."

It was stupid to keep the case open. After Horvath had left, Keegan felt bad about wishing his own stubbornness onto Horvath. Not that his deputy did not have plenty of his own. He would not be his deputy if he did not. Neither of them wanted to put all these files away and admit that, so far as the city of Fox River, Illinois, was concerned, Billy Murkin, alias James Dunbar, had been shot by person or persons unknown for undiscovered reasons and may God have mercy on his soul. The final sentiment might have been left to Roger Dowling, but Phil Keegan, once a seminarian himself, a daily communicant at St. Hilary's, was capable on his own of wishing Billy Murkin's soul well in the next world into which he had been propelled by one slug from a deer rifle, fired from an entry ramp five hundred yards away.

Dowling. Keegan wondered if Dowling would be interested in browsing around Dunbar's house while Keegan went, one last time, to see if anything had been overlooked.

After arranging with Dowling to meet him at the house, Keegan looked once more at the list of things that had been found on the person of Murkin/Dunbar when he died. Social security, credit cards, two for gasoline, a clipping from the Flanagan employee newspaper mentioning those who had worked for the company ten years, Dunbar's name just a name on a list. Driver's license. Money: $43.16 in cash. Only the general credit card was still valid and that was because it was not yet a year old. Dunbar had never used it. He had never used the others either, but they remained in his wallet, invalid. James Dunbar had not been an active member of the consumer society. Except when it came to booze. For all he drank, he seemed never to have been in any trouble because of it. He had no history of absenteeism, no traffic violations connected with drinking.

"He must have just sat down in his own living room and got stewed," Keegan said to Dowling. They were sitting at the curb in Dowling's car into which Keegan had slipped when the priest arrived.

"Or Mrs. Dunbar did."

"We figure both."

"Are we going in?"

"Horvath is coming with the key."

Dowling leaned forward and peered at the house. "Nothing special about it."

"No." It was all but indistinguishable from the other houses on the street, two-story frame houses, most of them stuccoed, the whole avenue a tunnel of huge elms that prevented sunlight from penetrating.

"That was an awful lot of booze for one person," Keegan said.

"Yes."

"And why the variety, bourbon, Scotch, the suggestion of cocktails. And all that beer."

"What did she die of?"

"Horvath is checking on that."

"Let's look around the yard."

The front yard was diminutive, scarcely twenty feet deep. When they went around the house, Dowling remarked on the narrowness of the lots. The next house was so close Dowling said he could imagine a man standing between them and touching each with his outstretched hands.

"It's hard to imagine people remaining strangers when they live so close. Didn't the neighbors have any gossip about the Dunbars?"

"If they did, they kept it to themselves."

"They must have noticed the bottles in the trash."

They had come around to the back of the house where

the yard was not much bigger than in front. A narrow walk led to the garage. Dowling went on to the garage and, cupping his hands, peered through a window.

"That door's open, Roger."

"Is that his car?"

"We brought it back here. It was parked down the street from the rectory. It's ten years old but in good condition. He drove it back and forth to work and had it serviced regularly."

"But not to church on Sundays?"

"You tell me. This is your parish."

As if to prove Phil Keegan's point, a woman in the next yard called Father Dowling's name. She came down from her porch, bare arms folded against the weather, a quizzical expression on her face.

"Hello, Mrs. Wenzel. I thought you lived on this street."

She came across her yard, arms still folded, as if she were carrying the burden of her breasts.

"Were you coming to see me?"

"This is Captain Keegan, Mrs. Wenzel."

"Oh, yes. I've seen him at Mass. Is there anything new on poor Mr. Dunbar?"

Before Keegan could answer, Dowling said, "You're going to catch pneumonia, being outside like that. For that matter, so are we."

"Would you like a cup of coffee, Father?"

"I certainly would. Phil?"

Dowling's Roman collar was an open sesame with which a police badge could not hope to compete, Keegan thought, as they detoured through the alley and into the Wenzel yard. Mrs. Wenzel, back on the porch, stood holding the door open for them.

"Now, promise you won't notice what a mess the house is in."

The house, as far as Keegan could see, was neat as a pin.

"Why don't we just sit here," Dowling said, pulling out a chair from the kitchen table.

"In the kitchen! Father Dowling, I may not be ready for company, but my front room isn't that much of a mess. You two just come with me and I'll have coffee for you in a minute."

But Dowling was already seated at the kitchen table. Keegan followed suit. Mrs. Wenzel fluttered about for a moment, then accepted it. She put cups before them. In her eyes was the look with which she would tell her friends that Father Dowling had just sat down in the kitchen, would not listen when she suggested the living room, such a simple man. The simple man now wore a grave look.

"What a shock it must have been to you, losing both of the Dunbars in so short a time."

"Isn't it awful?" Mrs. Wenzel plunked spoons on the table, her expression altered to the tragic role Dowling had just cast her for.

"First her, then a month later him."

"Isn't that often the way, Father?"

"Except that he was killed," Keegan said, cutting off the suggestion of some romantic bond that had tugged Mrs. Dunbar's husband into the beyond where they could once more be together.

"In my house, as a matter of fact," Dowling agreed.

"Such a sacrilege."

"Murder is always a sacrilege."

"Murder! The paper made it sound like an accident, a random shot." The coffee poured, she sank into a chair and looked at her two guests as if inviting them to philosophize about the precariousness of urban life. "Was it murder, Lieutenant?"

"It's Captain Keegan," Dowling corrected, avoiding Keegan's eyes. "Captain Keegan is in charge of detectives."

"Really?" Mrs. Wenzel adopted an expression of suitable wonderment. "Your men have been just crawling over that house. And they're not all gentlemen," she scolded. "The one who was here this morning was downright rude. I had to just plant myself in the doorway or he would have forced his way in."

"Did he give his name?"

"If he did I don't remember it. I didn't like his tone from the beginning. Not that I want to get anyone in trouble."

"What did he want to know?" Dowling asked.

"They all ask the same questions, Father. The questions Captain Keegan wants to ask me now, I'll bet."

"I'm sure you've answered enough questions," Dowling said. "It's not a very pleasant thing, talking about one's neighbors. I had to admit that I had never seen either one of them at Saint Hilary's."

"And now we know why, don't we?" Mrs. Wenzel's brow rose.

"I don't understand."

"Marie Murkin. She would have seen him and recognized him. Honestly, you think you know people, and then something like this. Imagine living so close to his wife, the woman he had abandoned, and neither of them ever meeting. Church apart, think of the opportunities. At the store, in the bus, at a service station, anywhere."

"But only he would have been aware of the risk."

"Yes." Mrs. Wenzel liked that. "He did have a sort of skulking look about him."

• 82 •

"What was she like?"

"Blanche? Nice enough. Not very communicative. She never warmed up. Years ago we used to talk a bit, in the yard, but then she got a clothes dryer and became almost a . . . What is the word?"

"Recluse?"

"Yes. Winter and summer in that house. Not that we get all that much sun in this neighborhood. The trees," she explained to Keegan.

"It appears they drank a lot," Keegan said.

Mrs. Wenzel put her cup in its saucer. She studied Keegan for a moment, then turned to Father Dowling. "I didn't think I should mention that. It seemed to be spreading scandal."

"I think it will be all right if you tell the police anything that might help them, Mrs. Wenzel. That isn't gossip. They have a job to do and we have a duty to help them. Did Mrs. Dunbar die at home?"

"An ambulance came, but from what I understand she was dead before they got her to the hospital."

"Was she sickly?"

"Well, you know she had diabetes."

"Were you in the house often?"

"Not in recent years. Oh, I know it sounds so impersonal, living side by side like this and not really knowing one another. I've felt so badly about it, particularly when I've been asked questions and haven't the least idea how to answer. But, Father, I really don't think we were to blame. We tried, we made an effort, and not just years ago."

"I'm sure you have nothing to reproach yourself for."

Keegan had never known Dowling to be so mollifying, but if it was studied, it was getting them nowhere. Dowling accepted for both of them when Mrs. Wenzel suggested more coffee. Keegan was not anxious to stay here and listen to this woman. It was when she was pouring the coffee that she said, "Look. There he is again."

Keegan got to his feet, expecting to see one of his men, if not Horvath himself, but the man who was approaching the Dunbar house from a car parked in the alley was not a member of the force. Keegan watched the man go up to the back door, bring out some keys and a moment later admit himself to the house.

"You've seen him before?" He was conscious of the plump form of Mrs. Wenzel beside him.

"He's the one I've been scolding you about. The rude one."

"I'll go over and talk to him. You'd better wait here, Roger."

"Roger? Oh!" Mrs. Wenzel blushed. "I'd forgotten that was your name, Father."

"Captain Keegan and I were boyhood friends."

Keegan closed the Wenzel door quietly behind him, crossed the yard, put one hand on the fence and vaulted over. In a second he was pushing through the back door of the Dunbar house. Once inside, he stood still and listened. Upstairs. What was he doing? He seemed to be walking from room to room, undecided. Doors swung on their hinges. He was making no effort to be quiet, but why should he?

There was the sound of the toilet flushing. The hall light went on and off. He might have been testing the facilities, a prospective buyer. And then there was silence.

Keegan waited. He might call out, there was no way the man could get out of the house from upstairs, but curiosity got the better of Keegan. He wanted to know what had drawn the man to this house.

He started up the stairs, slowly, trying to take as many steps as he could with each move, lifting his weight slowly so there would be no telltale creak. But the old house seemed to have creaks and groans that did not require a human foot to set them off. Motors hummed below, the furnace still going.

When he got to the landing, Phil could see the upper floor. No sign of anyone. Directly ahead was a bedroom. The last sounds he had heard must have come from there. The hall angled away to the right and that is where the bathroom was. The carpet on the staircase was threadbare.

He continued up, a step at a time now, cautiously. He could sense the other man's presence and suspected that his own had been detected. He took out his gun and held it close to his body. He did not want that to be the first thing anyone hiding upstairs would see. Using his head.

His neck too, as it happened. The hand cracked into the side of his neck and he fell forward, aware that his grip on the gun had loosened. It was the last thing of which he was aware.

15

AFTER Phil Keegan left, Roger Dowling sat on in Mrs. Wenzel's kitchen. He knew that Phil had thought him shameless, buttering up Mrs. Wenzel as he had, but it seemed an excusable way to prompt her to say what she knew of the

Dunbars. By now it seemed evident enough that she knew nothing of importance.

"How is Marie Murkin taking this, Father?" Mrs. Wenzel's voice was confidential.

"I only hope that you and I will show such courage if we are similarly tested."

"It must have been shatterng to learn that he had been living right here in Fox River all along. I don't know Mrs. Murkin well, but I almost feel that I was concealing something from her, living right next door to him and all."

"How could you have known?"

"That's it. It makes you wonder what other secrets are lurking around. People who look so ordinary and you find they've deserted one wife and taken another. I don't suppose the second marriage could really be a marriage."

"Not in the eyes of the Church, no."

"Well, thank God for Father Chirichi."

"Why do you say that?"

"I think he was a consolation to them, the Dunbars, certainly to her. She was very bothered by the fact that she was excommunicated."

"How did she put it?"

"It was not being able to go to communion, she said. She had very vivid memories of her first communion. But if she couldn't go to communion, she didn't see any reason to go to Mass. Do you know what she said to me, Father?" Mrs. Wenzel leaned forward and whispered. " 'I am damned', she'd say. 'I'm going to hell.' " Mrs. Wenzel sat back, her eyes rounded in horror. "You can see I couldn't say a thing like that with Captain Keegan here, even if he is a boyhood friend of yours."

"Of course not. What did you answer?"

"Answer? It wasn't a question, Father. It was a simple statement of fact. I mean in her own mind. What had she done, for heaven's sake? If we shouldn't make judgments like that on others, we shouldn't make them on ourselves either."

"Did you ever suggest she come talk to me?"

"Would it have done any good, Father?"

"Well, that's hard to say, of course."

"Now you know it couldn't have. We like you, Father. We like it that you're such a sensible old-fashioned priest. But that means you aren't going to tell someone in a bad marriage that everything is just fine. You're not going to pretend the rules can be bent all out of shape. Isn't that right?"

Father Dowling considered his coffee. Had Mrs. Wenzel summed him up fairly? She was right that he had no inclination to call black white, but he liked to think he had compassion. He could not accept the thought that he would not have been of help to Mrs. Dunbar.

"How did her husband feel?"

"I don't know. She only talked this way when we were alone, during the day."

"And when she was drinking?"

Mrs. Wenzel nodded. "She was a terrible drinker. All day long. Yet she never seemed completely drunk. She could always talk more or less sensibly."

"I do wish you had sent her to me. Or let me know."

"Father, what if she had gone to the parish house? Think of it. Two wives of the same man meet at Saint Hilary's rectory." Mrs. Wenzel made it sound like a droll story out of Boccaccio.

"What about Father Chirichi?"

"You know him?"

"I know who he is."

"Blanche wrote to him. I helped her with the letter, explaining her situation, saying how much she longed to receive communion."

"And he answered?"

"He came to the house. Drove right up in his van. They talked for a while, it was a Saturday and the Mister was home. He said Mass for them, right in their house, and she received communion. It had been years and of course she cried."

"Were you there?" Father Dowling tried to keep accusation out of his voice.

"She cried when she told me about it. I had noticed the van, of course, but who would have thought it was Father Chirichi?" Mrs. Wenzel paused. "Even if I had known, it was all kind of irregular, wasn't it, Father? After all, this is your parish."

"How long ago was this?"

"Several months ago. Was it terribly wrong, Father? Helping her write that letter?"

Father Dowling was saved the necessity of answering. Next door a motor roared into life and a car went spinning down the alley, gathering speed as it went. Mrs. Wenzel, too, lifted from her chair. "What on earth is that?"

Father Dowling went out the back and gained the Dunbar yard via the alley. As he ran, it occurred to him that there had been something odd in Phil's manner when he left. Dowling had assumed it was the look of a superior about to scold an underling. He opened the back door of the Dunbar house and stepped inside. There was a sound at the front door. Father Dowling waited. The sound of a key turning and then of a door opening. Father Dowling continued through the house and came face to face with Cyril Horvath.

"How did you get in, Father?"

"Captain Keegan came over here from next door. There was someone in the house. A car just drove away." It was odd that these true statements added up to nothing.

"Is he still here?"

"Phil? I think so."

"Captain Keegan!" Horvath bellowed. "Hey! Keegan."

There was a groan from upstairs and Horvath bounded up the steps. When Father Dowling reached the top of the stairs, Phil Keegan was seated on the floor, rubbing the side of his neck. He looked shamefacedly at Roger Dowling.

"Did you see who it was?" Horvath asked. He was more embarrassed than Keegan by what had happened.

"I know who it was. Help me up, Cy."

"Maybe you'd better rest some more. Who was it?"

"Cowper."

"Cowper!" Disbelief was added to embarrassment. Dowling had the distinct impression that Horvath would have preferred that he not be there to see Phil at such a disadvantage.

"Who is Cowper?"

Keegan got onto one knee and put his hand against the wall. Horvath got a hand under one arm and Dowling helped on the other side. Between them they got Phil Keegan to his feet. He was still very woozy.

Cowper, it emerged, was a former policeman who was now chief of security at Flanagan Construction. That it had been in a sense one of their own who had done this was obviously painful to both Keegan and Horvath. Father Dowling knew how they felt. Listening to Mrs. Wenzel speak of the ineffable Chirichi had given him a similar sense of being betrayed by one of his own.

Despite his condition, Keegan insisted on looking through the house. But meanwhile he sent Horvath out to round up Cowper. "I want him downtown. Assault, impeding an officer in the course of an investigation, obstructing an alley." He rubbed the back of his neck gingerly. "Causing a headache."

"I'll see if there's aspirin here."

Dowling went into the bathroom where the medicine cabinet proved to be a cornucopia of nostrums, prescriptions, bottles, tubes, sprays. Dowling surveyed the contents of the cabinet with awe. There was no aspirin, doubtless too pedestrian a remedy for the hypochondriac who had filled this cabinet. Most of the bottles proved to be empty and the majority had contained insulin tablets. He remembered being told that Mrs. Dunbar was diabetic.

"Find any?" Keegan asked from the hall.

"Look at this, Phil. Have you ever seen such a collection?"

Keegan came into the bathroom and looked at the contents of the medicine cabinet. He shook his head. "And not an aspirin in the bunch."

"They patronized different pharmacies." Dowling took an empty insulin bottle. Kunert's Drugs. Most of the insulin had been bought there. He knew Kunert's. It was in the neighborhood. The other things had come from discount stores. That seemed to be the principle: non-prescription items from discount druggists, prescriptions from Kunert.

In a bedroom closet they found Mrs. Dunbar's dresses, hanging all in a row, shoes beneath them. They might have been ghosts, their bodies gone. Dowling supposed there was nothing surprising in the fact that her things were still here; she had not been dead all that long. She was more present in the house than her husband. The closet that must have been his was all but bare. Two suits, one summer, one winter, a single pair of dress shoes.

"He would have worn work clothes," Keegan explained. "They wouldn't hang those up."

They were folded in a dresser drawer. Wash pants, work shirts, white cotton socks in abundance, the suggestion of a uniform in the combination.

A cupboard in the kitchen had served the Dunbars as liquor cabinet. And in the refrigerator were jars of olives and maraschino cherries. Bottles of mix. Bitters in the cupboard with the booze.

"Flanagan," Keegan mused. He was staring out a kitchen window.

"I beg your pardon?"

"Cowper. He worked for Flanagan. William Flanagan. You know him."

Roger Dowling, thinking of Eunice Flanagan, that puzzling girl, and mindful that what she had told him had been in confidence, was glad to be able to reply, without mental reservation, "I have never met him."

"In technical terms, he's a sonofabitch. Pardon my French."

"*Je vous excuse.*"

"What?"

"Two can play the swearing game. What possible relation can there be between this house and Flanagan Construction?"

"Dunbar worked for him."

"Even so?"

"Roger, you don't send your security man nosing around the house of an employee who has been shot unless you have a reason." Keegan was almost cheerful. "This is a break. Things are beginning to fall together. Don't ask me how. I don't know, not yet. But Cowper's being here means that we are not dealing with some damned chance occurrence."

16

AMBROSE CHIRICHI had come a zigzag course through thirty-two years to what he considered was a more or less definitive version of himself. The human person, not being a thing, could never be definitive. We are processes, not things. But, he thought, relaxed in the back of his van, his long legs stretched out on the deep pile carpet, his guitar as ever at hand, everything else is process too.

He struck a chord. On the stereo a classical guitarist was playing and he could only hope to chord in. We are processes not things and things are processes too. It might have been the theme for a homily, only he did not preach homilies anymore. Simplify. That was his goal. Simplify.

Simplifying had been a process too. Newly ordained, he had been assigned to an uptight suburban parish, its members so wealthy that the Sunday collections were an obscenity.

So gild the church, raise it higher; expand the school, build, spend. But the flow of cash rose ever higher and there were no more things to spend it on, so the pastor had begun to invest. The parish portfolio, of course, nothing personal.

"Why not give it away?" Cirichi had asked in his innocence. "Or stop taking it in. Tell them we've got more than enough. Tell them to give it to the poor."

Moriarity, the pastor, ordained thirty years, was not about to take this sort of radical nonsense from a young whelp like Chirichi ("What the hell kind of name is that?" he had asked, a smile on his lips, but a bit put out. "Indian?" Chirichi told Moriarity he was Italian. "A wop like the pope," is the way he had put it. He had not expected to get along with Moriarity and he was right.) The pastor explained the offertory, the gifts, the symbolism. "That money represents the fruits of their labor. It's important that they offer up some portion of it to God."

"We're not God."

"You say you're Italian. What about the Vatican?" Moriarity had gone swiftly to trump.

"Sell it," Chirichi had said.

Had he meant those things or was he just trying to get Moriarity's goat? But it was fruitless to keep examining motives, as if we are clockwork within; we are processes, not things—he knew that now. But he had not known it then. After an argument with the pastor, he had felt anguish. Moriarity had a legendary temper. Irish. When he blew his stack, it was completely. He became livid, irrational, unintelligible. He threw things. Once, after escaping from the room where they had been watching television, Chirichi had listened at the door while Moriarity smashed everything he could lay his hands on. He grabbed the cushions off the black leather lounging chairs and pitched them around the room.

Finally he threw a large glass ashtray at the TV and the picture tube went up with a great pop and lots of smoke.

Later Moriarity came to his room and told Chirichi he wanted him out of the rectory the first thing in the morning. He didn't care where he went but he was getting out of the house. "I'm sorry about losing my temper, but I know I'll lose it again if you stay here. You are the most infuriating person I have ever known in my life." Moriarity forced himself to stop. His coloring suggested that he would pop his cork again if he went any farther into detail.

Somewhat bemused, Chirichi had packed and gone to a motel. Several days later he phoned the chancery and told them Moriarity had thrown him out. Of course Moriarity had already gotten his version onto the record.

The inner city was next, what else? An Italian parish all the poverty anyone could want. All you had to do was stick your nose into the street and there it was, crime, hunger disease, extortion. Racism.

"You're a priest, not a real estate agent," Vitale the pastor, told him. "Leave these things to the laity. Our job is different."

"They hate blacks," Chirichi told Vitale.

"Why do you say that?"

"They won't let them move into this neighborhood.'

"So? That doesn't mean they hate them. How can they hate them if they don't know them? They just don't want them in the neighborhood."

"But that's not right."

"It's not wrong, Ambrose. It's not a sin. It's human nature. Like to like. Blacks are the same. We want to be close to our kind."

"We're all one kind."

Vitale nodded. "Sure. But not yet Here we re Jews

and Italians and Irish and blacks. It's not so bad God knows what he s doing. Lots of different flowers.'

Chirichi had continued his efforts. He talked some liberal whites from Loyola into signing leases for blacks, to get past the landlords. The neighbors were another story. Their anger had turned on Chirichi when they found he was behind it. A tricky black was one thing, but a priest from their own parish pulling a stunt like that? He was lucky to get out of the parish alive. Literally Vitale made him get into the trunk of his car and drove him to the chancery where he deposited him on the curb.

Chirichi did not go inside He picked up his bag and started walking. He ended up in Old Town where he got a job c erking in a leather store It was like summer vacation when he was in the seminary, time off for good behavior He informed the chancery where he was.

'You're not wearing clericals behind the counter, I hope?'

'No, Monsignor.'

'Keep in touch, Father Chirichi There is a spot for you and we'll find it."

"Maybe I have, Monsignor This is sort of a parish here "

He meant the people who roamed the streets of Old Town as it degenerated into a honky tonk after a valiant attempt to restore its alleged lost glory. The girls, the pimps, the hustlers of various kinds, the peddlers and users. Chirichi slept on a cot in a bare room at the back of the leather store, doubling as watchman. He thought, this is where Christ would be if he were alive today.

His own theology evolved from that thought.

At first he had not been conscious of the fact that he was deve oping a whole new concept of what it meant to be a priest, at least what it meant for him to be a priest. Living as he did, among the kind of people there, remembering the wealth of the suburban parish and the narrowness of the inner city parish, he resolved to stick to the essentials. To simplify.

He said Mass in the back room of the leather store at any time of the day or night. He substituted freely for the traditional bread and wine. He let anyone who wanted to share in the eucharist. If anyone felt unworthy, he had two points. We are all unworthy and as a priest he absolved them of their sins.

People came to him who thought they had turned their backs on the Church forever. Whatever their hang-ups, Chirichi overcame them.

"Forget it. You think Jesus cares about that?"

"Father Farley sure as hell did."

"I said Jesus, not Father Farley."

"He wouldn't let me go to communion."

That really frosted Chirichi. Keeping people away from communion. Jesus had become man to get in touch with everyone and priests withheld him and sent people away unfed. That wasn't right. A priest is supposed to forgive, not lay burdens on people.

And if someone tried to get him into an argument over whether Jesus had really lived, or really said this or that, Chirichi just smiled. Jesus was the name for what is good and peaceful. Not a man. The idea of God too could be accommodated to all sorts of things. People were meant to come together, not be divided by theories and rites and theology. Eventually the chancery sent someone to talk to him.

"We've been getting the strangest reports." He was a very young monsignor and he looked around Chirichi's room at the back of the leather store. "Do you say Mass here, Father?"

"Sure."

"But you can't do that. Not without permission. I don't believe you asked for permission, did you?"

Chirichi admitted that he had not. The litany of his misdemeanors went on. Listening, Chirichi knew he had reached a turning point. He was a priest. Nobody could change that. He did not need anybody's permission He was a free lance. He tried to develop the idea for the monsignor but without success. There was another visit and then he was informed that he had been suspended. But no one could stop him from being a priest. He had been made a priest irrevocably at ordination. That was one thing he and the people at the chancery agreed on. Once a priest, always a priest.

He won the van in a poker game. It was worth thirteen thousand dollars and was called Miss Lechery. There was a very explicit nude painted on the side. Chirichi loved it. It meant mobility. We are a process. He got around and wherever he went, people noticed he was there. There was a story on him, with lots of photographs, in the Sunday magazine section, probably run to irk the cardinal, which it did, but it also transformed Chirichi's ministry.

People came to him from all over. They wrote to him at the leather store. He did what he could. He went everywhere. Weddings, funerals, baptisms. Mainly he freed people from the fear that because they had broken some rule they were damned forever.

People like Mrs. Dunbar in Fox River. She had died without supernatural fears because she had written to Chirichi. He had assured her, a validly ordained priest had assured her, that everything was perfectly okay.

The tape on the stereo came to an end and Ambrose Chirichi took a sip of sangria. Next to kosher Concord, fruity and sweet, he liked sangria best. The van was parked in a trailer camp just outside Fox River. Chirichi liked the valley; he liked the people who lived here. He felt called to this place.

He no longer doubted his inspirations; they were clues to what he was, what he was becoming. We are processes, not things.

17

IT WAS ONLY after he decked Phil Keegan that Cowper recognized his old colleague and it did not seem a good idea to wait until Keegan came to and say he was sorry. In fact, the best idea seemed to be to get the hell out of the house fast. Which is what he did.

He was spinning down the alley before it occurred to him that Keegan must have seen him enter the house. If that was true, he would know who it was who struck him

Damn Flanagan anyway. Why couldn't he leave well enough alone?

The farther he got from the house, the surer Cowper felt that he should not have left it. He slowed to twenty miles an hour He pulled to the curb. He had to think. If Flanagan had been ticked off by the Dunbar memo, what would he do when he found out his chief of security was practicing karate on the Fox River police department's chief of detectives? There seemed little point in not finding out. Cowper put the car in gear and headed for the office.

Flanagan's secretary looked up frostily when Cowper burst into the outer office.

"Is he alone?" Cowper demanded.

"Mr. Flanagan is busy, yes."

Cowper repressed the desire to give her the finger. Deedee was one of those vestal virgins who give their lives to corporations, the demands of the office, the rituals of protect-ing their surrogate divinity from the rabble. He knocked once on Flanagan's door and opened it. Deedee, with a mild screech, rose from her chair. When Flanagan looked up from his desk, Cowper was standing in the doorway with Deedee hanging on his arm.

"He just flew past me, Mr. Flanagan."

"It's all right, Deedee. Come all the way in, Cowper. Just shut the door, Deedee. Thank you."

"Something's happened," Cowper said.

"I gathered that."

There was no way to tell it that did not make him look like a damned fool, but he had to give Flanagan credit. Wild Bill always began with the way things were, not with the way they might have been. He ran his thumb and forefinger along the bridge of his nose while Cowper told him about hitting Keegan, but that was all.

"Did he see you?"

"Not then."

"What do you mean?"

He must have seen me go in and followed me. I never

thought of a stakeout. Why the hell would there be a stakeout?"

"Good question. You might try to get an answer to it when you're being interrogated." Flanagan punched a button on the intercom and told Deedee to call the police. He wanted to talk with Captain Keegan.

"There is a policeman here now, Mr. Flanagan. A Lieutenant Horvath."

"Just a minute." Flanagan switched off. "Know him?"

"He's Keegan's right-hand man."

Flanagan depressed the button. "Send Lieutenant Horvath in, Deedee."

Cowper felt that he was being delivered up by Flanagan, but nobody could have prevented his having to go downtown with Horvath. Flanagan overdid the cooperative citizen role and Cowper marveled at his boss's lack of concern about his loyalty. When Horvath asked if Cowper was working for Flanagan at the time he was in the Dunbar house, Wild Bill was not fazed.

"Mr. Cowper works for me, yes. I don't imagine he ceases being my employee on his day off."

"Is this is day off?"

"Ask Mr. Cowper."

"We have a lot of questions to ask Mr. Cowper."

"That's fine. But I'm afraid you're going to have to do it elsewhere. This is my office, I am a busy man. I know that Mr. Cowper will be happy to assist the police in every way."

"He's a cool sonofabitch, isn't he?" Horvath said when they were walking out to his car.

"What's this all about, Cy?"

"Aw, come on, Leonard."

"Should I have a lawyer?"

"That's up to you."

Horvath did not head for downtown. Apparently Keegan was waiting for them at the Dunbars'. A chilling thought sailed across Cowper's mind. Had he struck Keegan too hard?

"How is Phil?"

"Nice of you to ask. Let him tell you."

Phil Keegan scowled at Cowper when he and Horvath came into the Dunbar living room where the chief of detectives sat with a priest.

"Welcome back," Keegan said. Despite the scowl, he did not seem too angry.

"Phil, believe me. I didn't know it was you until after I hit you. Well, a split second before I hit you. But it was too late then."

"Sit down. This is Father Dowling."

"You been getting the last rites?"

The priest smiled but Keegan did not. Nonetheless, collapsing on the sofa, Cowper felt relaxed. Keegan and Horvath he understood. He could have conducted this session himself. And that is more or less what he did.

"You want to know why I was here."

"I want to know why you took off like a rabbit after you assaulted me."

"What would you do if you found you'd just chopped the chief of detectives?"

"Why were you here?"

"Dunbar worked for us. Flanagan Construction. He had copies of keys we don't want floating around. Probate court couldn't help us, getting legal permission to enter the house would have been a nuisance, so I came here to pick them up."

"Why didn't you call me?"

"I had no idea you were interested in the place."

"No? Dunbar was shot, killed, maybe murdered. Of course we're interested in him."

"I meant the house. Why should you be hanging around here? Believe me, Phil, if I had had any idea it was you coming up those stairs . . ."

"Who did you think it was?" It was the priest. His tone was difficult to fathom, neither insistent nor casual.

"I don't know. I heard someone creeping up the stairs and then I saw a gun. The rest was instinct."

"Did you find the keys?" The priest again. Cowper was thrown off stride. The keys had occurred to him on the ride back with Horvath.

"Yes."

"Where are they?" Keegan asked.

"I turned them in."

"He was in Mr. Flanagan's office," Horvath said.

"You gave them to Mr. Flanagan?"

"Certainly not. I dropped them off at my office and then went to report what had happened."

"This is his day off, according to Flanagan."

"But you were here in an official capacity?" Keegan asked.

"Look, Phil, what the hell. The guy had company keys. He's dead, his wife's dead, there's no easy way to get them back. I told you, we can't have copies of our keys floating around."

"What were they keys to?"

"Various offices around the place."

"Do all employees have them?"

"Of course not."

"So Mr. Dunbar was a pretty important employee?"

"I don't know how important he was. But he happened to have these keys."

Keegan shook his head. "I don't like it, Leonard. What do you think, Cy?"

"He went straight to Flanagan's office when he got there."

"That's not true."

"His car was parked in a visitor's post right by the front door. The security office is in another building. He was going through the door when I drove into the parking lot. And he was moving fast. He couldn't have stopped off anywhere else and then driven to where his car was."

"Why are you lying to me, Leonard?"

"Phil, what the hell difference would it make if I was lying?"

"Why can't you tell me you gave the keys to Flanagan?"

"Because I didn't." Cowper, caught now, reached into his pocket and brought out a ring of keys. "I've still got them." It was the dumbest move he had made all day. But Flanagan would never forgive him if he involved him in this.

"Give them here."

"What!"

"Are those the keys you took from this house?"

Cowper's fist closed around the keys, his own; he could not turn them over. "No. You're right. I gave those to Flanagan." Maybe Wild Bill could think faster on his feet.

"I don't believe you."

"That's too bad."

"Yes. For you. Take him downtown, Cy, and book him. And remove his personal effects before you lock him up."

Cowper drew back his feet, measured the distance to the door while keeping his eye on Keegan. But at that moment the priest stood and walked across the room, cutting the path of exit. Infuriated, Cowper leaped up and tried to brush past Dowling, but the priest proved hard to move out of the way before Keegan and Horvath pounced. The handcuffs were the final blow.

"You've deteriorated, Leonard," Keegan said, shaking his head sadly. "You were a good cop once but you have deteriorated."

18

HER BROTHER Bob came for her in his pickup and he did not have much to say during the drive to the lawyer's office. Like his vehicle he seemed out of place in the city; his weather-worn face, like the rifle rack behind the seat, suggested open spaces, a rural setting. Marie Murkin thought that Bob was what Billy might have become, what he should have become: a farmer or a small-town businessman. The thought suggested a different lifetime than had actually been hers and thus, how-ever momentarily attractive, was fantastic.

"What is the lawyer's name?"

"Tuttle."

"Why did you choose him?"

"He was suggested to me by a fellow at police head-quarters. A man named Peanuts. He looked like a man you could trust."

"Tuttle?"

"No, Peanuts."

Tuttle, Marie decided, was not likely to be described as a man you could trust. He came across the room to greet them, pumped Bob's hand and shepherded Marie to a seat by his desk. Bob sat next to her while Tuttle, sighing theatrically, settled behind the desk. His smile died like a sunset when he gazed across at Marie.

"The deceased was your husband?"

"My estranged husband." It was a phrase used in the newspaper story.

"I see." Tuttle looked to Bob for help, but Bob, taciturn, suspicious, rustic, said nothing. "Just tell it to me in your own words," Tuttle said, his voice pleading. He shuffled the papers on his desk as if he was not sure what this appointment was for. Bob, having lit a cigarette, decided to speak.

"Her husband ditched her fifteen years ago. Just walked off. There was no divorce but he married another woman."

"And now he's dead?"

"He was shot," Bob said and Tuttle lurched. His eyes, set close together, seemed to cross in comprehension.

"Shot in the rectory?"

"No, in the head."

Marie looked at Bob. It was hard to tell whether he was making a joke or playing stupid. Tuttle nodded as if he had not found the remark at all strange. It was clear that he had all the reminder he needed as to why they were here.

"So here's the situation," he summarized some twenty

minutes later, taking into account the corrections Marie and Bob had made as he reconstructed the case. "Your husband lived illicitly with another woman now also dead. There is property to which you have a solid legal claim. There are no dependents, no other relatives who could possibly have a prior claim. Mrs. Murkin, our sole adversary is government. I'll check and see if the taxes on the house have been paid. I'll check first to see whose name it's in."

"I checked. It is owned jointly by Mr. and Mrs. James Dunbar." Bob lit another cigarette, his sixth.

"The alias. That's good." But Tuttle frowned. "And bank accounts, now. Where did he bank?"

Marie had no idea, of course, and neither did Bob. She was surprised that Bob had checked the title of the house. Did she really want to take part in this? The whole thing suddenly struck her as robbing the dead. What Billy Murkin owed her was too vast to be covered by a house and whatever other meager possessions he might have. She wished she had talked this over with Father Dowling, but Bob had made her promise to say nothing to anyone, as if hordes of people were getting ready to lay claim to Billy's house and they had to be first. Why did he care?

"Cause you're my sister and it's about time you had some good luck."

It had been a long time since anyone had shown that kind of concern for her. Marie melted. Going to see the lawyer was almost a favor to Bob, he was so intent on helping her. It would have been ungrateful to tell him that she did not want a red cent of anything Billy Murkin had owned.

"Where did your husband work?"

Marie found the question grotesque. "Mr. Tuttle, I had not seen that man for fifteen years. A few hours after I did see him he was dead. Killed. In my bedroom. It is very difficult for me to think of him as anything but a stranger."

"Psychologically, yes. I understand that. But legally he was still your husband. You never filed for divorce?"

"Certainly not."

"Good Catholic woman," Tuttle said. He was writing this down on the large yellow pad that never seemed to be out of his hand. "No more did he." Tuttle looked up. "Did he?"

"How could he divorce me without my knowing?"

Tuttle thought about that. He frowned. Bob said, "Does it matter?"

"He could not have obtained a divorce in this state, probably not in this country. Could he have obtained a Mexican divorce? Say he did. It would have to be in someone's interest to prove it. Who has such an interest? There are no other claimants. Except the government, the state government, who could . . . No. We have nothing to worry about."

But Tuttle's soliloquy bothered Bob. "Would he have a record of a divorce?"

"It is possible." But Tuttle had dismissed divorce as irrelevant and immaterial. "Now, where did he work?"

"Flanagan's."

"Flanagan Construction Inc.?" Tuttle's eyes crossed, then straightened. "That's good, very good. Employee benefits there are excellent. There should be an insurance policy, over and above the retirement benefits, I mean. Mrs. Dunbar, you are going to be . . ."

"Don't call me that!"

"I'm sorry. Mrs. Murkin."

"I don't like any of this. Bob, let's go."

Bob put a hand on hers. "It's yours, Marie. It's owed to you."

"That is right, Mrs. Murkin. That is absolutely right. I realize how painful it is, dredging up the past, but it is because of that pain that you must accept this small compensation for years of . . ." Tuttle let his voice drift off, as if the

English language had failed him, unable to serve up a term that could adequately express what Marie had borne these many years. Marie was finding Tuttle a very unconvincing man.

"Do you do a lot of this sort of thing, Mr. Tuttle?"

"My practice is a general one, Mrs. Murkin. I do not specialize. In law, as in medicine, there is too much specialization. I am a general practitioner, Mrs. Murkin, a family lawyer. I assure you that your interests are in capable hands. Who recommended me, by the way?"

"Peanuts."

Tuttle beamed. "Ah, Piannoni. The city councilman?"

"No, the cop."

Tuttle's smile dimmed. "The nephew. An excellent young man. Very well, Mrs. Murkin, I'll want an address where I can reach you. And a telephone number."

"I live at Saint Hilary's rectory. I'm the housekeeper there."

"Good. Of course." That went down on the yellow pad, along with the telephone number Marie reluctantly gave him. She imagined Father Dowling answering the phone. Would Tuttle be discreet?

"Lawyer/client communications are as sacrosanct as those between priest and penitent," he assured her.

"If a priest answers, it will be Father Dowling."

"I've heard of him."

"I'm not sure I even want him to know about this."

Tuttle twisted his lips with his fingers. He did not cross his heart. Marie got up and Tuttle circled the desk to the door. She did not like it when he squeezed her upper arm. After Tuttle shook Bob's hand they got outside.

"I don't like him, Bob."

"You don't have to marry him."

"God forbid."

While they drove to the rectory it seemed to her that for the first time she felt like a widow. Billy was dead. She was free. Marrying again was possible. But she could not imagine living with someone like Mr. Tuttle. She could not imagine living anywhere but in her cozy bedroom at St. Hilary's.

19

HALF A DOZEN priests from nearby parishes converged on St. Hilary's on the night Bishop Rooney administered confirmation. The clergy was a sizeable contingent in the procession entering the church after the *confirmandi*, whose families were already seated in the pews, Bishop Rooney in his episcopal regalia bringing up the rear.

The Mass was concelebrated and everything went without a hitch, thanks largely to young Turner, Rooney's master of ceremonies. At the actual administration of the sacrament, Rooney spoke to the young men and women with moving directness. Not a sermon, not a chat, just a vicar of Christ explaining to them the importance of the sacrament they were about to receive. He asked them to imagine the room to which the frightened apostles had withdrawn after Jesus left them a second time: a handful of nondescript men without talent, wealth, or education until, with a sound like a rushing wind and in the form of tongues of fire, the Holy Spirit came upon them. In a matter of minutes they burst into the street to declare the good news fearlessly. So too, Rooney said, in a manner proportioned to their lives, the young men and women of St. Hilary's must act after they received the Holy Spirit in the sacrament of confirmation.

Father Dowling, seated in the sanctuary with the odd sense of being a guest in his own church, looked out at the little class he had instructed in preparation for this event. They were a good sample of their generation, he was sure; they were a good sample of the church. He had come to know them fairly well during the weeks of instruction. Was it hopelessly unrealistic to think of them as soldiers of Christ? No doubt, like their elders, they would muddle through, falling, rising again, always, when they thought of it, resolving to do the great and noble deed later, when time and opportunity would doubtless be more favorable. Well, God loves us as we are and knows us better than we know ourselves. If He has chosen us, Roger Dowling had no desire to second guess Him.

Bishop Rooney had strolled into the center aisle and was questioning the confirmation class. He does it well, Dowling thought. There was no doubt that the red zucchetto on Rooney's gray hair added a fiery note of authority. Dowling did not know what to make of the claim that he and Rooney resembled each other. He certainly did not feel any special affinity to the auxiliary bishop. Rooney was a successful man, a good man, his record without blemish. Eventually he would be given a diocese of his own; he might go ever upward in the hierarchy. Father Dowling prayed that he himself would live out his life at St. Hilary's, and he had little doubt that the prayer would be answered.

When the bishop did the actual confirming, Father Dowling came forward to assist. Young men first, then the girls, presenting a slip of paper to Turner, who whispered the name that had been chosen. "James, receive the Holy Spirit,' while the sponsor lay his hand on the shoulder of the one confirmed. Following after the bishop, Dowling could see the expressions immediately after the reception of the sacrament, expressions of awe, of happiness, of awkwardness and distraction. Did they expect a physical sensation? He loved them all, these young souls for whom as pastor he was responsible.

Afterward Rooney mixed in the parish center, posing for photographs with a boy or girl who had been confirmed, achieving immortality in a dozen family albums. Dowling, keeping out of range of the cameras, was relieved to see that the Flynns seemed quite content with the proceedings. Bunny toasted him from a distance, holding a Styrofoam cup aloft. The visiting clergy, having tried the punch in the parish hall, went on to the rectory for a real drink. Dowling and Rooney followed after a bit. Having shown the flag, the other pastors were soon on their way, all but Salzman, and they settled down in the study.

"Well, Roger, that went very nicely. I congratulate you."

"It did indeed," Salzman agreed, dipping into his Scotch.

"Thank you, Bishop."

"I never see you at Forty Hours," Salzman said to Roger Dowling.

"I quit drinking."

Salzman was startled, then a bit angry. "Is that the only reason to go to Forty Hours?" He looked at the bishop, somewhat righteously. "Personally, I derive great strength from attendance at Forty Hours."

"Not many parishes are keeping up the practice," Rooney observed.

"Oh, we're pretty old-fashioned out here on the edge of the archdiocese, Bishop."

"I hope there's nothing old-fashioned about devotion to the Blessed Sacrament, Father Salzman."

Salzman smiled into his drink. "Do either of you remember Cashman?"

It was a prelude to a bout of reminiscing on Salzman's part, an exercise lubricated by several freshening trips to the Scotch. Salzman at sixty had a long clerical life to reminisce about and he did have a knack for anecdotes. Dowling found it difficult to appreciate Salzman to the fullest since he had hoped to reminisce with Bishop Rooney about their days on the marriage tribunal. There was no point in bringing that up while Salzman remained, if indeed it had been possible to deflect him from his own memories. Eventually, Salzman subsided. In fact, he fell asleep. Dowling and Rooney helped him upstairs to a guest room, the bishop absolutely vetoing Salzman's intention to drive home tonight.

"I hope you can accommodate more than one guest," Rooney said when they had Salzman settled.

"No problem. There's another room just across the hall."

"The thought of going back to Chicago tonight would be too much. Are you tired, Roger?"

"Not really. Would you care for more coffee?"

"I'd rather have brandy. Do you have some?"

"Of course."

"I didn't want to ask while Salzman was still up."

"He might have been up less long."

Rooney laughed. He came with Dowling into the kitchen while the pastor heated water for a cup of instant coffee.

"You have a good life here, Roger."

"Yes." He turned to Rooney. "Yes, I do."

For a moment, there was an almost envious look in the bishop's eye. He passed his snifter under his nose, inhaling. "No trouble with this?"

"No, thank God."

"Good. Tell me, Roger. Where was that man shot?"

"That was upstairs. In the housekeeper's room."

Rooney looked disappointed. "You retain the knack for being at the center of strange happenings, Roger. Who was it that did the shooting?"

"The police haven't discovered that. Come, my coffee's ready. If Mrs. Murkin hears us in the kitchen, she'll come down to serve us. Let's go back into the study." Settled there, Dowling went on. "The police have to face the possibility that it was just a random shot. Someone, a kid, a maniac, firing a rifle and perhaps unintentionally hitting Billy Murkin."

"What a world we live in."

"A random shot would be preferable to a deliberate one."

"I wonder. I honestly wonder. I suppose they've looked into the man's past to see what enemies he had?"

Roger Dowling gave the bishop a sketch of the police examination thus far. He regretted not having asked Phil Keegan to stop by tonight. Rooney would have enjoyed getting a police report from Phil.

"Have they considered that the marksman, whatever you call him, might have been aiming at you?"

"At me! Really, Bishop. The man was killed in the housekeeper's bedroom."

"Even so." Rooney had the expression of one about to launch a theory and Dowling stopped him. For a moment he had an intimation of what his own interventions must seem to Keegan. It was a sobering thought.

"Will you want to say an early Mass, Bishop?"

"Not too early, if you don't mind. The point of sending Turner back without me was to have a little time to myself. I'll take a train in tomorrow afternoon. What time do you say Mass?"

"At noon. Would you like to say yours then?"

"No, no. I don't want to interrupt your schedule. But I would like to get to bed now. I sometimes wonder, do people consider a bishop's life interesting?"

Dowling laughed. "I think they do."

"Roger, you would not believe the routine. I had more independence as a seminarian. It is not very often that the parish where I confirm has a pastor who is an old friend. This is the first time in months I haven't gone right back to town after a confirmation."

With Rooney settled in the second guest room, Roger Dowling had a final pipe in his own room, winding down. There was the faint sound of Salzman snoring down the hall. He felt tired himself. Poor Rooney. What must his life be like, confirmation after confirmation, feted and fussed over and passed on to the next parish? Dowling yawned. Marie must be buying decaffeinated coffee again. He would speak to her about that.

The following morning Dowling slept late and when he came down, Marie said that Salzman had had breakfast and gone. "What a grump," she said. "I think he had a headache."

"The bishop hasn't come down yet?"

"I haven't seen him."

He was not down an hour later and Dowling found it difficult to believe that Rooney had meant to sleep so late. He tapped gently on the guest-room door. No answer. He tapped again and waited. Finally he turned the knob and pushed the door open. The bed was empty. No sound from the bathroom. No sign of his clothes.

"Bishop Rooney?"

But a quick inspection made it clear that Rooney was not there. Dowling went downstairs and again asked Marie if she had seen the bishop.

"Is he missing?"

Dowling smiled. "Well, he's not in his room."

"Maybe he went over to the church."

It seemed a good idea until Dowling went over to the church and failed to find Bishop Rooney. Could he have gone back to Chicago already? It seemed odd that he would just go off. Or was it? For heaven's sake, he did not have to leave a note or make a speech. Had not Salzman just gone off without waking him? Dowling felt like a slugabed, his guests gone from the house before he even got up.

And yet he felt uneasy. The point of his uneasiness was clear when the phone call came.

"Who's that?" a voice asked insolently.

"This is Father Dowling."

"Cut it out."

"This is Saint Hilary's rectory and I am Father Roger Dowling."

"I said cut it out. We got him. Now listen. Here's what you're going to have to do to get him back."

Dowling sat down. His first impulse was to regard it as a joke. But then, as if he had known it all along, he was certain that this caller had somehow gotten Bishop Rooney into his control under the mistaken impression that he was Roger Dowling. It seemed best not to insist on the error he had made.

"I want fifty thousand dollars."

'That's absurd. I don't have fifty thousand dollars."

"Who is this?"

It seemed an inspiration when he said it. "This is Bishop Arthur Rooney."

"No kidding?'

"Why are you holding Father Dowling?"

"I want fifty thousand dollars. Make that a hundred thousand dollars. You say you're a bishop. The Archdiocese of Chicago can afford that."

"How do you want it?"

"I don't want it. That's not it. I want a hundred thousand dollars worth of food distributed to the poor."

"Where is Father Dowling now?"

"He's right here with me."

"Let me talk to him."

"He'll be all right, just so long as that food is distributed. Here's how you do it."

Dowling listened, angry and distracted, to the elaborate scenario the insolent caller outlined. He wanted maximum coverage by television and the newspapers. People had to be told that the demand had been made and shown that it was being met.

"You got that?"

"Yes, yes. Now let me talk to Father Dowling."

His answer was a click as the line went dead. Without hesitating, Dowling began to dial Phil Keegan's number. In the back of his head a remark of Rooney's the night before repeated itself. Maybe he was shooting at you, the bishop had suggested.

20

PHIL KEEGAN was listening to Hogan from the prosecutor's office tell him that there was not a chance in hell that they would bring action against Leonard Cowper.

"Morrissey has been reading me the riot act and I don't blame him. What the hell did we arrest Cowper for?"

"How about breaking and entering?"

"He had a key."

"Where did he get it?"

"What if he claims that Dunbar gave it to him? They work together, they're friends."

"Is that what Cowper's saying now?"

"It's what he could say and then what do we have?"

"Assaulting an officer of the law."

"The difficulty there, Phil, as you must know, is witnesses. It is an inference on your part that he struck you. You didn't see him do it."

"He admitted it in front of witnesses."

"Did he? Maybe he did but he sure as hell isn't going to make a dumb admission like that while Morrissey is representing him. Do you know that Morrissey is seriously considering a false arrest charge?"

"I'm frightened to death."

"Phil, listen to me. This could be serious."

"You listen to me, Hogan. Dunbar was shot to death. Dunbar wasn't even his name. He was a runaway husband, a bigamist. Something funny is going on and what the hell was Cowper prowling around his house for?"

"Prowling is your word."

"He said he was after keys. I have witnesses to that, Hogan. Horvath was there. Father Dowling was there."

"I'd keep quiet about Father Dowling if I were you. Flanagan really went up the wall when he heard Dowling was interrogating his chief of security."

"Interrogating?"

"That's his word. And what about the Dunbar shooting anyway? Do you have anything on it?"

That was the unkindest cut of all. Not that he thought of Hogan as being on his side. Life was tough enough without having Hogan on his side. But the prosecutor's office should not be against the police either.

"I'll let you know."

"You're not getting anywhere, are you?"

"I said I'll let you know."

It was not a good mood to be in when Roger Dowling called to say that someone had kidnapped Bishop Arthur Rooney. Keegan let Hogan get out of his office, waited until the door closed, before speaking. "I'll be right over, Roger."

Being at the rectory did not help him to understand what had happened. That familiar house, always a pleasant place to visit as respite from the pressures of his job, looked different now. A man had been shot there and now a bishop had been kidnapped from it. Or that was the assumption. No one had seen a goddam thing. Marie Murkin was near tears when Keegan asked her for the fifth time to please concentrate. Had she heard anything at all suspicious?

"Captain Keegan, I've told you. No."

"All right, Marie. All right." He pushed his cup toward her and she refilled it. "Let's not lose our minds. Just tell me everything you did from the moment you woke up until Father Dowling came down and asked you if you had seen Bishop Rooney."

So she told him, in detail, but none of the details told him anything. Marie was not going to be any help at all. Had she talked with Father Salzman while he ate? She had not. The priest was surly and hungry and anxious to be on his way. Where had she been while Salzman ate? In the kitchen. Had she gone outside at all? She had taken some trash out to the garbage can. What time was that? Back and forth, they tried to establish the time when Marie Murkin had taken out the garbage and Keegan could not believe that it mattered one way or the other. Marie had not heard anyone drive up. Had she heard Salzman drive away? No. His car had been parked in the lot next to the parish center. Dowling came into the kitchen and Keegan turned to him almost with relief.

"Father Turner is on the phone, Phil. He's expecting Bishop Rooney. Rooney has a full schedule this afternoon and Turner is getting a little nervous."

"What did you tell him?"

"Nothing so far."

"I'll talk to him."

"Phil, the cardinal has to be told."

"You want me to do that?"

"I'd better. I'll tell Father Turner too. He may take it easier from me."

Roger might have been Turner's informant but whoever had called the rectory had telephoned the cardinal's office too. As soon as Dowling put down the receiver, the phone began to ring. Keegan ran upstairs and got on the extension.

"How long do you suppose they'll remain under the illusion that they are holding you and not Bishop Rooney, Father Dowling?" an unmistakable voice was saying.

"I have no idea, Your Eminence. It was foolish of me to identify myself as Bishop Rooney. At the time, I somehow thought they would know he had spent the night in the rectory. In retrospect, I can see that was wrong. There was no reason they would have known that."

"I would have heard from them in any case. I don't imagine you have half a million dollars lying about loose, have you?"

"Is that what they're asking for now? They started with fifty thousand dollars."

"They want the poor fed. I explained that I do not require force to accept my obligation to feed the poor."

"You refused?"

"Not at all. I shall indeed give the equivalent, in food, not cash. It is not a new departure for the Archdiocese of Chicago, Father Dowling."

Listening on the extension, Keegan wondered if the kidnappers would be satisfied with that. Sure, the archdiocese had all sorts of social programs going, but what was demanded was something special, something dramatic, and something that would include mention of why it was being done.

"Have you informed the local police, Father Dowling?"

"Your Eminence," Keegan said. "This is Captain

Philip Keegan of the Fox River police. I am on an extension. Father Dowling phoned my office and I am here now trying to get a lead on what happened."

"You've been listening in, Captain?" But there was a chuckle in the cardinal's voice.

"We are monitoring all calls, Your Eminence. In case they call again."

"Good. I trust you will use the utmost discretion, Captain Keegan. Nothing must be done that would jeopardize Bishop Rooney."

"Then I think you are going to have to stage the extravaganza they are demanding, Your Eminence. You're going to have to have a televised giveaway and it's going to have to be made clear why you're doing it. I can appreciate that that rankles, as if you needed instruction in charity from kidnappers, but, after all, it's the poor who will benefit. But tell me, how did the caller identify himself to you?"

"He didn't give a name."

"Did he mention an organization? A cause?"

"Nooo. Are you still on, Father Dowling?"

"Would you like me to get off the line?"

"Not at all. I have had a thought as to who might be behind this and I wonder if you couldn't provide Captain Keegan with the background. You know of Ambrose Chirichi, do you not, Father? Fill Captain Keegan in on him. It is the best I can do by way of a lead."

"What do you think, Roger?" Keegan asked, when he had come downstairs. Dowling was seated at his desk, staring straight ahead. He looked at Keegan.

"Do you know Chirichi?"

"I've read about him."

"The cardinal could be right. He has been in the vicinity. Phil, Chirichi buried Mrs. Dunbar."

"Dunbar!"

Dowling nodded but he had no more idea as to how the crazy events of the past few weeks hung together than Keegan did. Phil Keegan telephoned downtown, got Horvath and told him to have research come up with a package on Ambrose Chirichi. He put his hand over the phone. "How the hell do you spell Chirichi, Roger?"

Keegan repeated it as Dowling spelled it. "Cy, there was a story on him in the *Tribune* Sunday magazine a while back. Call them and find out when. I want a copy of that article. It had lots of photographs. Photographs of the van he drives around in."

21

Bob Fletcher nosed the pickup right up to the garage doors, hit the horn with his elbow when he got out, slammed the door, and stood beside the truck, stretching. That done, he lit a cigarette and looked with vague resentment at the Dunbar house. He shrugged, whistled, got his toolbox out of the back, slung it over his shoulder, and let himself in through the gate. In the next yard, a woman was hanging out clothes and watching every move he made. Bob headed right toward her, got his toolbox rested on the fence, and smiled at the world.

"Morning, ma'am."

"Hello. No one's home there, you know."

Bob laughed, loud and long. "If they was, that'd be what they'd be wearing, wouldn't it?" He pointed at the sheet the woman was pinning to the line. She did not laugh but her manner changed. She finished with the sheet and came over to the fence. The pockets of her apron were filled with clothes pins. Wooden ones.

"They're just clothes pins," she said, in response to his exclamation of surprise. She handed him one. Her suspicious manner was back.

"Just clothes pins! You try buying any like this lately? Plastic. That's all you can find. Plastic clothes pins. These are the kind my mother used to use."

"My mother did use those."

"See? They last forever." He leaned across the fence, but his eye was on the sky. "Longer than people. Too bad about those two, huh?" He hunched a shoulder at the Dunbar house.

"Did you know them?"

He settled for a chuckle. This time he hunched his other shoulder, toward the pickup. "We got to keep the place in repair. In a nice neighborhood like this. Your husband must be quite a handyman." He cast an admiring glance at the woman's house.

"This is a very good neighborhood, for an older one."

Bob assured her that, so far as he was concerned, the older the better. Where were you going to find houses built like these nowadays and, if you did, which you wouldn't, how much did you think you'd pay for one? Yet houses like these, in their day, had gone for what we'd now consider a song.

Mrs. Wenzel—they had exchanged names by now—said that they had paid fourteen thousand dollars for their house. In the fifties, she added vaguely. On to mortgages and interest rates then and to the disturbing news that it was now difficult to get a mortgage on houses this old.

"Well, I'd better go inside and look her over," Bob said. He dropped the cigarette he had been smoking into the brownish grass. Would winter never end? He decided against broaching that subject. The weather was inexhaustible.

First he reconnoitered, walking the perimeter of the yard, studying the house, now and then stopping to take off his cap and scratch his head and frown. From time to time, he wrote things down in a little tablet he carried in his shirt pocket. He noticed the tags spinning from the door knobs indicating that the house was sealed. He entered by a basement window, stepping from the washtubs to the floor and, after a quick glance around, went upstairs.

This was the enemy's camp and he muttered as he moved through the house. The sonofabitch. The sonofabitch. This is where he had been holed up all those years, living like everyone else, Marie just blocks away working her fingers to the bone, waiting on priests, a grass widow. Why the hell hadn't he at least left the town? Marie had grown old with nothing in her life while Billy holed up here with another woman. They had all assumed he had gone to California or to Florida, some place that would be an improvement over Illinois, some place that sounded like a vacation, since that is what Billy had taken, a vacation that lasted a lifetime.

"If only you had come to me sooner we could have gone through that house like a dose of salts," Tuttle had complained.

"You figure that's where it is?"

"There could be a safety deposit box. That is not easy

to find out, not easy for you or me. I doubt it. What do you think? Would he be likely to rent a box in a bank to put his valuables in?"

"They're in the house," Bob decided.

"Well you should have come to me sooner." Tuttle's informants—Peanuts?—told him that the house was now an object of interest to the police.

"Why?"

Tuttle looked mysterious. "I learned long ago not to search the doings of the police for rhyme or reason. Someone doubtless had a hunch."

Bob would have preferred rhyme or reason. Hunches he understood. "They damn well better still be interested in that house,' he-told Tuttle.

"Your friend's killer will be caught," Tuttle assured him.

"That sonofabitch was no friend of mine."

"Even so," Tuttle said, alarmed by his vehemence. He began to tap his fingers on the chaos of papers on his desk, as if there might be a keyboard concealed there somewhere and he in need of mood music to go with the pensive expression he now wore. "I could—mind you, this is merely a statement of fact, not of intention—I could engage someone to enter the house on your behalf, look around . . ."

"I'll do it."

"Now, Mr. Fletcher, I can't advise a client to do a thing like that."

"I know. I know."

"But you're going to do it?" There was a devilish expression not far off, ready to be plucked from Tuttle's bag of facial masks.

"No need to announce it."

He sure as hell did not intend to pay someone else to

look through the house to see what insurance policies or other valuables Billy Murkin might have acquired over the years. Tuttle could do the obvious checking, at Flanagan's, where Billy had worked, but hire someone to look in the house and who knew what valuable and negotiable stuff might disappear in the process?

Bob found what he was looking for in the dining room, in the china closet, under a pile of napkins and table cloths. A stiff paper envelope, tied with a sort of shoelace and, printed across the flap, Valuable Papers. He pulled out a chair from the table and sat. It was not easy to untie the string while wearing work gloves. It was difficult to tell about the stuff inside the envelope, fancily engraved papers with the color of money. Bob received from Reader's Digest advertising gimmicks that looked as good. But he soon saw that these were insurance policies. He put them back in the envelope, retied it and stuffed it inside his denim jacket. In the basement, he thought better of that and transferred the envelope to his toolbox. He hesitated before getting onto the washtubs.

Was there more stuff here? He would like to go over the house from top to bottom, but he had already spent forty-five minutes since parking his truck out back and there was no point in pushing his luck too far. He boosted the toolbox out the window, then boosted himself. It was a bit of a strain, he was not as young as he used to be.

Nor did it ease the strain when the man waiting for him held out a hand and offered to help.

22

COWPER extended one hand to the man emerging from the basement window. In the other hand, he held a gun. He was not smiling although he had every reason to.

It was about time things started going his way. Leaving his number with Mrs. Wenzel and offering her twenty-five dollars if she would call him should anyone other than a cop show up at the Dunbar house had been one of those long shots he had been losing as consistently as more reasonable ones. But luck runs in streaks and Cowper knew his was due for a turn and here it was.

"We'll take the toolbox with us," he said to the man. "I'm parked out back."

"So'm I." An idiot grin. He hitched the strap of the box over his shoulder, using just his thumb. Given what that box must weigh, Cowper decided against relaxing. This guy was wiry and strong and maybe not so dumb either.

On the way to the car, Cowper pocketed his gun, keeping behind the man with the toolbox so that he would not notice and get ideas. Once through the gate and out of sight of Mrs. Wenzel—she had been peeking over her laden clothesline like an old picture of Kilroy—he got out the gun again and ordered the man into his car.

The man swung his toolbox into the bed of the pickup and went around the car.

"Wait," Cowper snapped. The man looked at him across the hood of the car with gray unblinking eyes. He might have been an animal.

"You drive," Cowper said.

The man shrugged and came back. He slid behind the wheel and Cowper slammed the door. He got into the back seat himself and reached across to put the keys in the ignition.

"You're not a cop," the man said.

"Who are you?"

"Where we going?"

"Just drive where I tell you to."

"Like hell. Have you ever used that thing?"

Cowper made a menacing gesture with the gun, put the barrel between the man's shoulder blades and pushed. The man leaned forward and Cowper pulled the wallet from his back pocket.

"From out of town, huh? What do you do, drive into Fox River and break into homes?"

"Now tell me what you do."

"I'm in security work. Private."

"Who hired you?"

"I'll ask the questions. What were you after?"

"Whatever it was, I didn't find it."

"Why the toolbox?"

"To fool the neighbors. Ask the old lady next door. She thinks I came to keep the place in repair."

Cowper frowned. "For who?"

"For the owners." But the man had hesitated. There was something going on here. Cowper opened the door and stepped out. He wanted that toolbox.

No sooner was he out of the car than it roared into life and began to back into the alley. At first Cowper could not believe it, but he had left the keys in the car like a damned fool. He stood there, holding the gun, his mouth wide open. The guy, Fletcher, had slammed on the brakes and was shifting. And then, by God, he started right for Cowper. Cowper danced out of the way, but the man swerved toward him as he moved, and the fender nicked his thigh and then there was a crash as the car struck a corner of the garage.

Immediately the maniac threw it into reverse and was swinging back into the alley. Cowper darted toward the yard. He raised his gun but he could not bring himself to take a shot at his own car, one fender of which was now a mangled mess. Cheerist! He was coming back again. This time Cowper hopped onto the pickup but that did not stop the bastard. He rammed into his own truck. Infuriated now, Cowper grabbed the strap of the toolbox and with one motion hurled it at the windshield of his car through which that sonofabitch was grinning up at him. The car had started to back off and the toolbox hit the hood with a plunk, making a huge dent as it sank into the metal. With the toolbox on its hood, the car wheeled away into the alley. This time it continued to back down the alley toward the far cross street.

"What on earth is going on?"

It was Mrs. Wenzel from next door. She held a towel up before her, a reluctant Salome down to her last veil, but the sight of the gun in Cowper's hand contorted her face with surprise.

"It's okay, lady. It's okay."

Cowper hopped down from the bed of the truck and

stepped cautiously into the alley. The grill of his car was just disappearing as it turned into the street. A second later, the car shot past in profile, the toolbox still on its hood, and Cowper went off down the alley on the run, waving his gun, raving and cursing as he went. Goddam it anyway. Why hadn't he remembered those keys in the ignition? Just to get the damned toolbox, he had let the guy get away. Wild Bill would hit the fan when he heard of this. If he heard of it.

Putting away his gun, slowing to a walk, Cowper tried to think. There had to be a way out of this. He could take a cab to the office, call the police and report the car had been stolen.

It was not much of an idea, but it was the best he could come up with. It might have worked too if the police car had not nosed into the alley before he got to the street. Cowper ran toward the vehicle, watching the hood dip as brakes were applied. The back door sprang open and a German shepherd flew out and came for him, fangs bared and emitting a growl that made Cowper's hair stand on his head. He tried to stop, but slid in the gravelly alley. He got an arm up before him, waiting for the dog to leap. But the cop was out of the car now, in control of the dog.

"Get your hands over your head, join them on top, don't move."

"Did you see my car?" Cowper yelped. "Somebody just stole my car."

The cop came forward and began patting Cowper's chest. A moment later he plucked out the gun. "Back to the car. Slowly. Fritz is well trained but he does not like surprises."

"Officer, for Christ's sake! Somebody just stole my car. You must have seen it. There was a toolbox on the hood."

The cop glanced at him. "What is it, a collector's model?"

He had his mike out now and Cowper heard himself described as a very excited civilian, armed, who had been terrorizing the neighborhood. Unless the code had been changed, he was being described as a nut. How could he deny it?

"Officer, do me a favor, will you? Check out that pickup parked up the alley. You want my ID?"

But going for his billfold activated Fritz and he crouched.

"Fritz," the cop commanded.

Cowper, lurching, let go of the wallet. The dog snapped it up and gave it to the cop. Too late, Cowper saw that it was not his own wallet that he had taken out.

"Okay, Mr. Fletcher," the cop said. "Let's go."

23

THE NEWS that an auxiliary bishop of the Archdiocese of Chicago had been kidnapped from the rectory in a parish in Fox River where the night before he had administered the sacrament of confirmation was the premier item on local and national broadcasts. More emphasis was put on the demand that had been made for the bishop's release than on anything else, which seemed reasonable enough since half a million dollars destined to feed the poor was clearly more newsworthy than a single prelate whose elevated status suggested that he had not missed many meals lately.

Interviews with the cardinal were sought, but the networks had to settle for the vicar-general, himself a bishop, who tried to review the extent and amount of the archdiocese's involvement in the amelioration of the plight of the poor.

"Why won't the cardinal meet with the press, Bishop?"

"He is meeting you through me as his spokesman."

"Shouldn't he speak for himself?"

The questioner's insolence was occupational, Roger Dowling thought, turning off the TV; it was merely the accusative tone of his trade. He himself had to deal with lesser pundits, Mervel of the *Fox River Messenger* and Ninian a stringer for the *Tribune*.

"Bishop Rooney was your house guest, Father Dowling?"

"That's right."

"Did he have any premonitions of what happened?"

"Of being kidnapped? I rather doubt it, Mr. Mervel."

"What I'm after, Father, is human-interest stuff. The mood of the bishop, what was he doing, the final hours of freedom of Arthur Rooney, that sort of thing."

Father Dowling tried to oblige, to the extent that his conscience permitted him to. He realized that Bishop Rooney was becoming a mere pawn in the game of publicity, a faceless figure, the hostage. How benumbed we are by the violence and atrocities of our times. Arthur Rooney, held by someone, was unlikely to regard his office as a shield to protect him. Anyone who would thus force another person about against his will was apt to do anything.

"Father Dowling," Mervel said, rubbing the side of his

nose with the eraser end of his pencil. "Why was your name used in the first message received?"

"The *Messenger* received a message?"

"I think we may have been the first ones contacted." Mervel sat a little straighter.

"That suggests he is being held in Fox River, don't you think?"

Ninian said, "The *Trib* and other Chicago papers were also contacted. And the cardinal."

"That's true."

"We nearly ran a story you were being held, Father Dowling." Mervel laughed.

"That would have been embarrassing."

"The wire service saved us."

That seemed odd to Dowling, local news being read from a ticker. Where did it originate? "I could have corrected that," Dowling said.

"We couldn't get through to you. The line was busy."

Dowling shunted the two reporters off to Marie Murkin. He had not been alone since the discovery of the bishop's absence. Did it matter that at the beginning the bishop had been mistaken for Roger Dowling? He recalled that it was Bishop Rooney himself who had suggested that the pastor of St. Hilary's might have been the intended target of the shot that had killed Billy Murkin. Had there been two attempts on him, both of which had gone awry? That seemed unlikely, but of course what was truly unlikely was the notion that anyone would want to kill or kidnap Roger Dowling.

The kidnapping, surely, had been enhanced rather than thwarted by the apparent mistaken identity. A bishop made a far more impressive hostage than a mere priest. If he himself had been the target, there would be a unity of theme currently lacking in the dramatic occurrences at St. Hilary's rectory. Roger Dowling was a constant element. Both Billy Murkin and Bishop Rooney had been unlikely occupants of the house at the time the events occurred, particularly Billy Murkin. There seemed to be no motive whatsoever for shooting Billy Murkin. Why not assume then that Billy had not been the intended target?

"Who else?" Keegan asked. He had told the girl to bring Roger Dowling right in to his office but now he looked regretful.

"Me."

"You!"

"Think of it, Phil. Both the shooting and the kidnapping took place at my house. The kidnapper actually thought it was me he was holding hostage."

"But that turned out not to matter. Besides, if someone first wanted to kill you, why would he settle for a kidnapping? Have you got any enemies?"

"Have you?"

"I don't imagine that people are after me."

"You have incurred animosity merely by doing your work. Don't you suppose the same is true of me?"

"Roger, at the moment we are following up on the cardinal's suggestion."

"Chirichi? That might make sense so far as demanding that the cardinal distribute food goes. Admittedly, that has a Chirichi touch to it. But Billy Murkin?"

"You're the only one who thinks the two go together, Roger."

"You like coincidence as an explanation even less than I do."

"Very well. Murkin is Dunbar. You told me that Chirichi had something to do with the Dunbars. What was it? He buried her."

Dowling nodded. "That's right."

Keegan shrugged and showed his palms but Roger Dowling was not impressed. Perhaps Phil thought that he was trying to dramatize himself, but that was not it. Phil knew that Roger Dowling was a connection between Billy Murkin's death and Bishop Rooney's kidnapping. The motive? The person or persons involved? He did not know. But it was something, it was a great deal, to know the nature of the problem, and the problem now was: Who had wanted to shoot Roger Dowling and, failing that, to kidnap him?

These thoughts were interrupted by Horvath's call. Chirichi's van had been spotted, parked in a trailer camp north of Fox River.

"Stay with it. I'm coming out. No radio contact. That van has CB and all the rest."

"How did you know that?" Dowling asked as they went downstairs to Keegan's car.

"I read it in the *Tribune*, Roger." He pulled from his pocket the folded pages of the magazine story devoted to Ambrose Chirichi. "You can read that on the way to the trailer park."

24

CYRIL HORVATH was Phil Keegan's good right arm largely because all he had to be given was the hint of a direction and he was off in single-minded tenacious pursuit. The *Tribune* article had been more than sufficient to guide him. Not only were there many photographs of Chirichi, there was a series on his van, the Miss Lechery, with shots of its somewhat sybaritic interior, its radio equipment, its stereo. All this was due to its previous owner, the man from whom Chirichi had won the vehicle in a poker game. What interested Horvath was the license number. He was able to give it out to the state police and the Fox River department and was himself on the way to Old Town when a Fox River squad car reported that the van was in a local trailer park. Horvath ordered the patrol to continue surveillance until he got there. On his arrival, he verified that the plate was indeed that of Chirichi's van. The vehicle looked like an old friend because of the newspaper article. After phoning Keegan, Horvath took up the vigil, wondering what precisely they were going to do.

Was the missing bishop in the van?

Assuming that he was, Horvath began to devise ways of taking the vehicle with a minimum of danger to its occupant. Despite himself, the confusion he had felt reading about Chirichi crept back into his mind.

The man was a priest. He lived in a van. He had won the van playing poker. The poker game had taken place in the back of a leather store in Old Town. Old Town was a legendary place, from a policeman's point of view, not at all where one would expect to find a priest. Horvath did not understand it. In the article, Chirichi had made much of the fact that the way he lived was the way Christ had lived, the people he associated with were like the friends of Jesus. The statement had a specious truth. Had Jesus played poker? Did Jesus tool around in a van? As far as Horvath knew, a priest's job was to say Mass, baptize, officiate at weddings and funerals, all this in church. Chirichi had no church. According to that article, he had just walked away from his last assignment for which, eventually, he had been suspended.

Suspended. It sounded like being hanged. It certainly hadn't cramped Chirichi's style. He had just gone on living as he had before. How could the church stop him from doing what he did? They could not. For that matter, there was nothing to stop anyone from just starting his own religion and setting up shop pretty much where he felt like it. Not only would he break no statutes, his right to do so would be protected by the Constitution. Horvath found this confusing. But Chirichi was, or at least had been, a priest, a real priest. He should know better, Horvath thought.

But it was that background that made the possibility

that Chirichi had snatched the bishop and was holding him hostage in the van a live one. A grudge. He would be getting back at his old bosses by making them dish out a huge sum of money with nothing to be shown for its going than some smiles on the faces of the people who had received the food. Smiles that would be gone tomorrow when the food was gone.

The van was painted black with orange trim and a nude on the side. A small port window toward the rear. Horvath had ascertained that no one was up front. The curtain behind the driver's seat was pulled; the port windows, bulbous, distorting glass, gave no clue from a distance as to what if anything was going on inside. There was no rear window.

It was now eleven in the morning.

Horvath came alert at the sight of a bearded man slouching his way toward the van from the supply store/restaurant, the only immobile home in the park. Chirichi. He was shorter than Horvath had expected. He had the look of a man who has just eaten well. As he walked, he unwrapped a cigar and, at the van, the cigar in his mouth, he lit it. One foot up, one foot down, he puffed contentedly at the cigar, the blue-gray smoke hovered for a moment and then trailed away. Chirichi surveyed the world. Was he as nonchalant as he appeared or was this a survey of the terrain, on the lookout for signals of danger? As the gaze of Chirichi swung toward him, Horvath felt increasingly identifiable as a cop. Who else would be parked like this, doing nothing, obviously on stakeout? In peripheral vision, he kept Chirichi in view. When the door of the van opened and Chirichi with surprising agility piled in, Horvath turned his head toward the van.

A motor started. The van? He could not tell. But suddenly the van began to move, to move rapidly, making a U turn and heading into the trailer park. Horvath twisted the key and got his car going, but Chirichi was out of sight behind some mobile homes before Horvath got moving. He swung into the park and, in a stroke of luck, caught sight out of the corner of his eye of the van emerging from the park He slammed on his brakes, backed into the street and was in good position behind the van before it really got moving. How easily he might have gone groping around in the trailer park while Chirichi disappeared.

He could see Chirichi in the van's side mirror and he seemed to be using it to check his tail. Horvath picked up his mike and told the dispatcher to hook him up with Keegan. He was not surprised when Keegan told him to apprehend Chirichi.

"You think he's got the bishop?" Keegan asked.

"Could be," was all Horvath was willing to venture.

Almost immediately the sounds of sirens became audible. The van slowed, hesitated, and Horvath passed it and nosed into the curb, forcing the van over. He got out quickly, armed, not wanting any fast back ups. If Chirichi tried it, Horvath was prepared to shoot out the front tires.

But Chirichi had bounded out of the van and now padded up to Horvath. Horvath, expecting anger, was surprised by the serenity of the man's expression.

"Police," Horvath said, showing his badge.

"Clergy," Chirichi said, showing his teeth.

Other police cars began to arrive and Chirichi looked around, puzzled. "What's going on?"

"You alone in the van?"

The priest brought an index finger to his own chest. "You're really after me?"

"Your name Chirichi?"

"What have I done?"

"Let's take a look in the van."

"Of course we can look in the van. What are we looking for?"

A moment later, Horvath was glad he had not answered that question. The van was empty. He avoided Chirichi's eyes. "Just routine."

"Routine? You're kidding." Chirichi's teeth glistened in a smile and then he laughed. He began ostentatiously to count the police cars that had gathered. Eight. And then Keegan pulled to the curb in front of Horvath. Father Dowling was with him. Horvath shook his head, to let Keegan know. Chirichi was frowing at the man in clerical clothes.

"I'm Roger Dowling. You're Chirichi, aren't you?"

"What are they looking for?"

"Bishop Rooney," Dowling said without hesitation. "He's been kidnapped."

To his credit, Chirichi did not pretend that it was unthinkable that he might have been the one who had caused Bishop Rooney to disappear from St. Hilary's rectory. He even seemed a little disappointed that he had not thought of it. "Food for the poor," he mused. "That's good, Father Dowling. That's good."

"May I see your van?" Dowling asked and Chirichi, pleased as punch, led Dowling off to show him Miss Lechery. Horvath turned to Keegan.

"It was possible."

"Yeah."

"He even acted suspicious."

"Can you believe that guy's a priest?"

"No."

Keegan shook his head. "Dowling had an idea, Cy. He may be right. What if all this has been aimed at him, the shooting, the kidnapping? A comedy of errors."

Horvath could not tell how seriously Keegan took the

possibility. It was not likely, but then neither was a shooting and a kidnapping at the same address. He decided that Keegan took it seriously when he told him to keep an eye on Dowling.

"Protect him?"

"We don't want anything else to happen. Be inconspicuous about it, all right? I wouldn't want him to think I believe him."

25

"I WON IT in a poker game," Chirichi said.

"So I've heard."

"Do you approve?"

"Of winning at poker? Certainly. What would you have lost if you hadn't won?"

"A lot of plastic chips."

Roger Dowling, seated in a swivel chair, turned slowly, taking in the interior of the van. "You sleep here?"

"It's my home," Chirichi said.

"Well, I can't say I envy you, but it seems nice enough."

'Father, did they really think I kidnapped Bishop Rooney?

"Did you?"

Chirichi peered at him. "You're serious?"

"Yes."

'No, I didn't. How did you get involved in this?"

"The bishop was staying in my rectory last night. Saint Hilary's, here in Fox River."

"I wonder who did it."

"No ideas?"

"Father Dowling, I like the idea of putting the screws on the archdiocese, to feed the poor. But I couldn't condone kidnapping. I am against any kind of violence."

"The kingdom of heaven suffers violence."

"And the violent bear it away. But what does that mean? That they put it out of reach, hide it, kidnap it?"

"How did you come into contact with the Dunbars?"

Chirichi seemed to think before his whiskered mouth formed an O of comprehension. "I've been poaching? I didn't charge a cent for the funeral."

"Was that all you did?"

"How do you mean?"

"The Dunbars' marriage wasn't valid."

Chirichi considered his cigar. "Validity, jurisdiction, laws, rules. That's what drove me out."

"Is it? They serve to distinguish out from in, I suppose."

"God is love," Chirichi said, sending a series of smoke rings sailing through the van.

"Do you miss the priesthood, Father Chirichi?"

"I still have it. You know that."

"I mean priestly activity."

"That too. I still have that."

"But the Mass?"

"Father Dowling, I can say a valid Mass. And I do."

"But a licit Mass?"

"No one can take my priesthood away from me."

"We only exercise it in communion with the bishop, as his aides. You know all that."

"I knew it, maybe. Doesn't it bother you that love gets all wrapped up in roles and laws? That's bad enough for just ordinary things, but it's a scandal to think we can control the flow of God's love."

"A scandal?" Dowling said, his eyes going around the plush interior of the van. Curious faces appeared at the port-hole windows and people were standing around on the sidewalk. The police cars were going away but Keegan and Horvath remained. Phil came through the crowd and poked his head into the van.

"I'm leaving, Roger. Coming?"

"Could you give me a lift home?" Dowling asked Chirichi.

"Sure. Sure."

Keegan waved and went. Chirichi turned in his chair, facing the wheel. He locked the seat in place, waved and smiled at the onlookers, started the engine. It purred, the promise of power. Having consulted the rear-view mirror, Chirichi pulled into traffic.

Roger Dowling gave directions, turning slowly back and forth in his swivel chair as they drove. Poor Chirichi, he seemed a decent, confused young man. What sort of a life was this, living in a van, rootless, without function? He might regard himself as a free-lance priest, but there is no such thing and Chirichi should know that if he did not. He recalled a conversation with Bishop Rooney. His old friend had mentioned the *episcopi vagantes,* validly consecrated bishops without dioceses, ordaining others, on the fringes, and however much they might disdain the rules and regulations, they relied on them conscientiously in the matter of ordination, the apostolic succession, passing on the priestly function from generation to generation with an essential link to those Christ had chosen as his first ministers. Chirichi, too, clung to the memory of his ordination as the basis for his otherwise self-defining activity. Was there any chance of urging him back to where he belonged? Mercy and forgiveness came easily nowadays. A repentant Chirichi could be back in a parish in a matter of weeks. Roger Dowling suggested this, as if thinking aloud.

"You looking for an assistant?"

"Saint Hilary's scarcely keeps one man busy."

That was the problem, of course. What pastor would welcome Chirichi to his parish? The prodigal son. That lovely story, the parable of God's inexhaustible mercy, stood vividly before Roger Dowling's mind. He would offer Chirichi lunch. The fatted calf.

The faith is a paradox. Of course it must not be reduced to rules and laws, but neither could it be volatilized into what you will. The balance of opposites. Love bound by rules. It seemed an image of marriage, and marriage had always provided the best metaphor of the soul's relation with God. Limits imposed by a free promise were not constraints on love.

At the rectory, Marie had the noon news on TV and waved them in to watch. Bishop Rooney had retained his hold on the Number One spot. An archdiocesan spokesman, perhaps the same one Roger Dowling had heard earlier on radio, requested prayers for the safety of Bishop Rooney. Plans were going ahead for the purchase and distribution of food. "Under religious auspices?" a questioner asked. The spokesman was nonplussed. "The food is being distributed at this time and in this manner under duress. Those are the auspices."

"Have you heard anything further from the kidnapper?"

"I might ask the same of you. I am told that several newspapers and television stations have been contacted."

The scene at the chancery became a silent film as, in voice-over, an announcer said that this channel had indeed been contacted by the kidnapper. A face appeared to match the voice and several minutes were devoted to recounting the telephone call. The message had a virulently antireligious tone. And then the news was over.

"This is Father Chirichi," Roger Dowling told his housekeeper. "He will be my guest for lunch."

Chirichi came with him to the church and, from the sacristy, followed Roger Dowling's Mass. They walked back to the rectory in silence. Inside the house, Chirichi inspected it as Roger Dowling had inspected his van. "So it all goes on," he said. "Nothing changed. Business as usual."

"Mass, the sacraments, the usual thing. Of course. Why not?"

Chirichi seemed about to launch into a speech, but he held himself back, settling for a smile. "Why not?"

"Any vocation can come to seem dull," Dowling said, when they were seated at table and Marie had served. "Personally, I am more than content that one day should seem pretty much like another. I imagine there is a sameness even in your nomadic days."

Chirichi ate with relish, as if it had been some time since he had eaten the kind of food cooked by Marie Murkin.

"Do you have a family, Father Chirichi?"

"You don't have to call me that, Father Dowling. I don't need the title."

"As you said, you are ordained. I address your priesthood with respect."

"Touché."

"Do you?"

"A family? No. A brother I never see, he lives out west. That's all."

"Your parents?"

"Are you seeking the cause of my behavior?"

"Good Lord, no. I know the cause."

"Free will?"

"Free will."

"I like you, Father Dowling. You are a fixed star in a swirling chaos."

During the meal, Marie came to whisper in his ear that someone had parked a bus in front of the rectory with an obscene picture on its side. Father Dowling told her not to worry about it.

"I'll take care of it," Chirichi told her.

And so he did, after lunch. They shook hands before parting and Roger Dowling asked Chirichi to return.

The young man smiled. "You'd like to rescue the prodigal, wouldn't you?"

"That goes without saying."

Sometime later, Roger Dowling received a puzzling telephone call from Mr. William Flanagan.

26

TUTTLE hustled Bob Fletcher right out of his office and into his car and drove circuitously for ten minutes before pulling up to the rear entrance of a skid-row bar. He entered first, running the punishing gamut of a narrow passageway that went past fetid rest rooms to the bar itself where the smell of Lysol vied with that of stale beer. Tuttle slid into a booth whose high-backed benches concealed their heads from the people in the adjoining booths. Tuttle waved away the scabrous waiter but Bob called him back and ordered a bottle of beer.

"Make it two," Tuttle said, as if by way of concession. When the waiter was gone, he said, "You struck gold?"

Bob Fletcher nodded.

"Show me. No, wait. Wait till after he brings our beer."

"I was caught coming out of the house."

"What!"

"I went in through the basement window and when I came out again a man with a gun was waiting for me."

"A cop?"

"He said he wasn't. He wanted me to go with him."

"What did he look like?"

"Tall, heavy. He didn't smile much."

"That could be Horvath. What happened? How did you get away from him?"

Their beer arrived and Tuttle stopped Bob's narrative until the waiter had shuffled away, talking to himself as he went. Bob resumed his story and Tuttle's eyes started from his head.

"You're pulling my leg," he pleaded. "This didn't happen."

"Sure it did. The woman next door must have seen it all. I think she's the one who blew the whistle on me, the bitch. And I was so nice to her before I went inside."

"You showed yourself to the woman next door?"

"Well, how do you mean that?"

"Stop joking! Do you realize that you've made an ass out of Cyril Horvath?"

"You're sure that's who it was?"

"From your description."

"I don't think he was a cop, Mr. Tuttle. I mean, he acted pretty dumb. And all he did was wave that stupid gun around. Why didn't he use it? A cop would have used it, right?"

"Who else could it be?"

"Search me."

"Did this man search you?"

"I told you. But he wouldn't have gotten the stuff. Even if we had driven away, the policies were in my toolbox and he let me throw that onto the truck."

"You said you drove away in his car."

"Drove right around to the front of the house, plucked the toolbox off the hood and cut through the yard to my truck. The lady next door had gone in, I guess. Anyway, I didn't see her."

"Why do you keep mentioning the lady next door?"

"Because I was nice to her and I think she called that guy and told him I was in the house."

"That's an inference."

"Of course it's an inference. What the hell's wrong with that?"

"Let me see the policies."

Bob plunked them onto the table and Tuttle scooped them up as if they were a hand in poker. Down and dirty. His eyes lit up as he examined what Bob had found "The jackpot," he cried.

"So you were right about insurance. What about Flanagan's?"

"They have a retirement plan. But it operates in a zillion different ways. I can't find out what option Dunbar took without making a direct inquiry."

"Murkin."

"What?"

"His name was Murkin, not Dunbar."

"The retirement plan would be in the name of Dunbar."

"Okay. But when we talk about him he's Murkin."

Tuttle sipped from his bottle of beer, avoiding the cloudy glass that had been served with it. "Now, if there are securities somewhere, in a safe-deposit box . . ."

"You're sure my sister won't have any trouble collecting on those?"

"I give you my solemn assurance. This money will be your sister's." Tuttle began to stuff the policies into the inside pocket of his suit jacket.

"Give them to me," Bob said.

"I have a safe in my office."

"I'll take care of them. I risked my neck getting them and I don't want them out of my sight."

"But where will you keep them? In your toolbox?'

"It's probably as safe as your safe. No, I'll put them where they can't be found."

"That's what I'm afraid of."

"What's that supposed to mean?"

"Life is a fragile thing, Mr. Fletcher. ·Consider the Dunbars. Murkins. Murkin. Your sister's husband and his wife." He gave up. There seemed no appropriate way to put it. "What if something happened to you? Where would your sister find those policies?"

"Nothing's going to happen to me."

"Famous last words, as the saying goes. Mr Fletcher be sensible. We'll put the policies in my office safe If any thing happens to me, there they are."

Bob had by now put the policies inside his denim jacket. "They'll be safe with me."

Tuttle obviously did not like it, but what could he do? For the first time, Bob Fletcher faced the fact that he did not really trust Tuttle and he regretted having gone on about the way he had broken into Billy Murkin's house. That knowledge in Tuttle's hands· was worse than the woman next door witnessing the break-in and worse than the guy with the gun. He was certain that Tuttle was wrong in thinking him a cop.

27

COWPER sat in his cell staring at the floor. He had been there too long already and he did not think that he would be soon released. Flanagan would be pissed but proper now and he could not blame him. Cowper had the mordant certainty that this would cost him his job, or it would if he did not know where the bodies were buried. A security man's security is all the dirt he is privy to in the line of duty. Even personal things, like Wild Bill's daughter.

The hell with Wild Bill's daughter. Cowper wanted to get up and grip the bars and shake them, assuming the classic pose of the unjustly accused. Even his demand to see Keegan had been ignored. He had counted on Keegan's getting a kick out of seeing his old buddy Cowper back again, sitting in a cell, particularly after what Morrissey had managed to do with that assault charge. Keegan had never really forgiven him for leaving the force.

"Moonlight if you have to," he had advised. "But stay on. Think of the years on your pension you'd be throwing away."

But Flanagan had promised to cover that; his pension at Flanagan's dated from when he had joined the police department, not from when he had joined the company. At that time, Flanagan was just starting to get his really big contracts and he had reason to fear that competitors would begin to play dirty pool, send people in after hours to examine his estimates and thus be able to underbid him with ease. Flanagan knew that game, because he played it himself. Cowper was to insure that Flanagan never became the victim of the method that had put him on Easy Street and kept him there.

The trick had been to use people other than the guards and watchmen. Only he and Flanagan had known who their man was. Dunbar had volunteered himself, indirectly, not quite saying it. The fact is he had done his first job on his own, bringing the results to Flanagan. Flanagan called in Cowper. Wild Bill was delighted so Cowper hid his resentment. That soon, less than a year on the job, and his position seemed in jeopardy. Dunbar had done what Flanagan expected of Cowper, had done it as a lark and brought home the bacon. But Dunbar had not been after Cowper's job. He wanted to stay right where he was, fooling around as an expediter, to all appearances a man without talent or ambition, content to be one rung up from the bottom of the ladder. During the day. At night, Dunbar was in and out of the offices of competitors like a cat.

From then on, Cowper had dealt with Dunbar, grudgingly admiring the man's skill. Flanagan could not be seen with his spy. If he could have managed it, Wild Bill would have liked the whole operation to go on without his knowing about it, just getting the results, underbidding where it was profitable, enjoying his reputation as the shrewdest contractor in the business. It had come as close to that as it could. Flanagan did not have to give explicit orders; Cowper knew the competition, he knew what Flanagan needed. And Dunbar knew too.

Dunbar knew. Despondent in his cell, humiliated, Cowper was able to admit to himself that his job had been dependent on James Dunbar. Dunbar had sustained him. Flanagan did not need Cowper to supervise the guards and watchmen; any number of people could have done that part of his job. What Flanagan was paying him for was the stolen information that enabled him to flatten his competition in bidding for the jobs he really wanted. And Dunbar was the man responsible for that information.

Of course Dunbar had been paid well, getting a fair percentage of the bonuses Flanagan had passed on to Cowper, in cash, tax free, a bonus indeed. Living as modestly as he had, Dunbar must have been salting it away, all those years on the gravy train, all income, no outgo. The guy had to be loaded.

But no one is ever sufficiently loaded, it seems. Cowper had learned this sad truth in his own case. The effort to convince Flanagan that he had a stable of people gathering information on rival bids had not worked. Flanagan had known that he, like Cowper, was dependent on only one man. The fact that Wild Bill used Cowper as his intermediary did not mean he had gone soft in the head.

"What does he do with the money?" Flanagan wanted to know. Of course he thought Dunbar was getting more than he was, but what Dunbar was actually getting was enough to make it an interesting question. And Flanagan had not liked the answer.

"It's better than having him flaunt it. I mean, on his

salary he can afford to live the way he lives. He starts driving big cars and taking fancy vacations and questions arise."

"Yes," Flanagan mused, and Cowper could have kicked himself. He might have been describing himself. And then Flanagan said, "We're the ones who are hooked on him. We need him more than he needs us."

"What can we do?"

Flanagan gave him the fisheye. "You tell me."

But if there was a move to be made, Dunbar made it. And it was a beauty. Cowper got it from Flanagan to whom Dunbar had brazenly gone.

"He's got records of every operation. Microfilms." Flanagan shoved a piece of film across the desk. "That's the sample. He can show that the record of Flanagan Construction is built on the theft of bids from rival firms."

"Anybody can take pictures of old bids."

"Take a look, you idiot."

But Cowper could not make out the picture. Flanagan explained it to him. In it Wild Bill Flanagan was pictured holding the incriminating evidence. "How'm I going to explain sitting around reading the bids of my competitors?"

"What does he want?"

"He's not going to get it," Wild Bill growled.

Dunbar was not going to wait patiently for Flanagan to make up his mind either. It soon became clear that intelligence was traveling in the wrong direction. Flanagan lost several bids he had very much wanted. His information about his rivals was false. It became difficult to ignore that one, Cronstrom, had correct information about the Flanagan bid.

Whatever arrangements had been made between Flanagan and Dunbar, the threat had lifted. Dunbar had gone into retirement. From industrial espionage, that is. He continued to work as an expediter. His wife was ailing. His wife died. And, when Dunbar himself was dead, Flanagan told Cowper he wanted more assurance than he had paid for that there were no more microfilms. He wanted anything Cowper could find that might suggest the kind of work Dunbar had really done for Flanagan Construction.

Cowper had not been acquitting himself well in this effort.

He had kept away from the Dunbar house while the police still seemed interested in it. His contacts downtown suggested that they had turned up nothing that excited their interest. And then he had moved, too soon, and there had been the embarrassing encounter with Keegan in the upstairs hallway of Dunbar's house.

Morrissey had gotten him out of that one, but Cowper did not see what plausible story could explain his running down the alley waving a gun and scaring hell out of the neighborhood.

Not that he was fearing a charge.

What he could not believe was that Phil Keegan would overlook the intensity of the interest he had shown in the Dunbar house. Cowper, Morrissey. The police were going to be led on to Flanagan. And it was Wild Bill Cowper feared.

He could not lose his job.

But his job could lose him.

Look at what had happened to James Dunbar.

A door slammed, a tuneless whistle was audible and Cowper looked up to see Cy Horvath. "You keep coming back like a song." Horvath tried to sing it, without notable success.

"Let me talk to Keegan."

"You scared him, Leonard. He's afraid you'll give him another chop on the neck."

"Don't, Cy. Please. You don't know what it's like to be in one of these goddam cells."

Horvath's face was not an expressive one, but it altered enough to suggest sympathy. He cracked no more jokes. He whistled for the guard and got the door open.

"Your wish has been granted. Come on."

Cowper went off after him like a kid being taken to the principal. But it was a helluva lot easier than facing Wild Bill Flanagan was going to be.

Keegan did not look up when Horvath led Cowper in and sat him down. The sheet Keegan was reading would be the report.

Cowper said, "Some bastard heaved a toolbox onto the hood of my car and then stole it."

"That's a year-old Olds, black, whitewalls, license 32154?"

"You found it?"

"Parked in front of the Dunbars'. Badly dented hood. Toolbox?"

"One of those big mothers, with a shoulder strap. He swung it like a slingshot." Cowper liked that. He sat back in his chair.

"David and Goliath?"

"Sort of."

"What were you doing back at that house?" Keegan yawned. "And don't tell me you were looking for keys."

"Did you find those too?"

"Aw, come on, Cowper."

"Two small flat keys on a beaded chain. I carry them in my pocket." Cowper turned the side pocket of his jacket inside out, displaying the little coin pocket under the flap. "I figure they had to pop out when I was running out to the car. I better start at the beginning. When I pulled up behind the Dunbars', there was this pickup already there."

"Robert Fletcher," Keegan read.

"How would I know his name?"

"That's the name in the wallet you dropped in the alley in the course of being arrested."

"Keegan, this is as embarrassing as hell."

"Try telling the truth."

"I'm telling you. I got there and there's this pickup parked behind the house. Out-of-town plates, from the southern part of the state. The lady next door tells me the driver is in the house. The doors are locked. Sealed. I find an open basement window. So I just waited and apprehended him when he came out."

"You apprehended him."

"This is the embarrassing part. He gave me his wallet when I asked who the hell he was. That was when he got up onto his truck, to get his toolbox."

"Why?"

"He'd put it there when I marched him out to my car and then, since he'd had it with him in the house, I decided he should bring it along."

"Where?"

"Here. I was arresting him. That's when he just flung the damned thing onto the hood of my car. Scared the hell out of me. I got rattled. And he was agile as a cat. The next thing I know, he's backing down the alley in my car, going like a bat out of hell. I gave chase."

The stilted phrase dropped like a rock in the silent room. Neither Keegan nor Horvath said anything.

"What did you say his name was, Phil?"

"Fletcher."

"That's your man."

"Did you ever find your keys?"

"What? No, I never did." Cowper smiled sourly. "I got arrested."

"'Get out of here."

"You mean it?"

"Get the hell out of here, Cowper. And don't ever show up again."

He could not believe it. He was on his feet and at the door, Horvath with him, in a split second. They stopped for his personal effects, all but the gun, they could have the goddam gun. He held his car keys tight in his fist, a little boy on his way to the store, and not even the sight of his car could entirely remove his feeling of euphoria. Cars can be fixed. He wheeled out of the police garage, a smile on his face, a citizen again, free as the breeze.

Fletcher. Robert Fletcher.

Who the hell was Robert Fletcher?

28

Mrs. William Flanagan was worried about Eunice but Bill, when she reached him, was so distracted that she had been unable to convince him that there was a basis for concern.

"She is twenty-four years old, Zoe. She's a big girl now."

"She has been a big girl for some time now, Bill. And she has been a cause for concern for some time too. As you very well know."

"Not now, Zoe."

"She did not come home all last night. She has given up the apartment, so she can't be there. Where did she spend the night?"

"Zoe, I mean it. Not now!"

He hung up. She sat staring at the phone. Such rudeness was not like Wild Bill. She rose, ran her hands over her hips, blinked several times and stared at the window. She was in the den, the room where Bill worked at home. When he was not at the office, he was working at home. Such a driven life he led, work, work, work, and for what purpose? What are we here for? On the slate of her mind, a passage from the catechism formed. Why did God make me? God made me to know Him, to love Him, to serve Him in this world, and to be happy with Him forever in the next. If that simple sentence summed up the purpose of life, it seemed an ironic commentary on what their lives had become.

Was it silly to think that they had been happier when they had less money? Wild Bill had worked as hard or harder, but he had not been estranged from her and from Eunice then. He had shared with her the ups and downs of the business, even though she had not understood a word he was saying. There had been gloom then, but there had been joy as well. Now there seemed to be only a desperate compulsive working. And they got richer and richer.

She was convinced that money was of little or no help in raising a child properly. They had sent Eunice to all those hoity-toity schools—Catholic ones, it is true—but she was a spoiled pampered child who had never wanted for anything, who had no real conception of how difficult life was for the majority of mankind. Mrs. Flanagan sighed, her sigh the romantic longing the rich can feel for penury. Oh, to be poor and free of these burdens. The unburdened poor would have been surprised by such reveries, but they were too busy being poor to notice. Or did they notice the use of denim and burlap in *haute couture,* the fifty-dollar imitation of the workman's shirt worn by business executives?

Zoe wandered through the house and upstairs to Eunice's room. Standing in the doorway, looking into the room, so bright, clean, and unlived in, she could not help crying. Eunice seemed determined to leave no trace of herself here, and it was not just the house. Her apartment had been the same. It might have been a display at a home show, impersonal, anyone's.

The books here dated from Eunice's time in college. Zoe took one from the shelf. St. Augustine's *Confessions.* Flipping the pages, she found no trace of Eunice's passage through them. But no. She paged back. A passage had been scored with a yellow marking pencil. The opening sentence of Book Eight: "Now my evil abominable youth was a thing of the past." Mrs. Flanagan stared at the sentence in horror. Did Eunice regard her youth as evil and abominable? What other significance could there be to the marking of the sentence?

Mrs. Flanagan remembered having come upon her own mother once at prayer and feeling a similar vertigo. Of course she had been used to the sight of her mother kneeling in church or leading the family rosary in May, but on this occasion Zoe had come quietly upstairs, glanced into her parents' room, and seen her mother kneeling beside the bed, her face in her hands. It had been just before noon, she recalled it vividly. Why should the sight of her mother praying fill her with terror, almost with dread? That suppliant figure, so creaturely and vulnerable. Was that it? Zoe had never been able to say, but the image remained with her. Her mother as contemporary, like herself a mere child so far as God was concerned. And now Eunice's adoption of Augustine's assessment of his past life filled her with a similarly unwelcome emotion.

It had never before occurred to her that the explanation of Eunice's lethargic indecision in recent years might be connected with religion. But of course! Father Dowling.

Mrs. Flanagan went swiftly downstairs. Before leaving the house, she wrote a note, saying where she was going. To whom was it addressed? Did anybody care? And then she went out to her car.

It had been some time since she had been in the section of Fox River where St. Hilary's parish was. The new roads and freeways had crisscrossed the city, the city itself had fled to the four winds, regrouping in suburban enclaves. Yet, once within the triangle that contained the parish, she found it reassuringly as it had always been. Unchanged. Older homes, yet they seemed in good repair.

St. Hilary's church, Neo-Gothic, brick, stood like a piece of the past claiming the gray sky as its own. Mrs. Flanagan parked in front of the rectory and, having turned off the motor, remained behind the wheel. What would she say? Would Father Dowling even be at home? With a sudden impatient movement, she opened the door and stepped out. This was no time to rehearse a speech. She was a distraught mother, worried about her daughter, anxious to see the priest who had warned Eunice not to marry Andrew Pilsen.

"Is that what Eunice told you?" Father Dowling asked.

He was a man in middle life whose leanness made him seem taller than he was. Thin face, penetrating eyes, an expression that put her immediately at ease. If she had come in with a set speech, she was sure she would have discarded it as soon as she met Father Dowling. He had taken her down the hall to a parlor, seated her, and then settled behind the desk. How long had it been since she had seen a priest in a Roman collar, let alone a cassock? Like the neighborhood, Father Dowling seemed a reassuring link with an earlier, better time.

"I'm not criticizing you, Father. My husband made some inquiries about the Pilsen boy and I was quite relieved when Eunice said that you were against the marriage."

"What kind of inquiries did your husband make?"

"I never asked."

"Would he have hired anyone?"

"He has enough employees as it is."

"Did your husband tell you of our conversation?"

"You talked with Wild Bill!" She smiled. "That's what he's called."

Father Dowling nodded. "I think I know why."

"Surely he wasn't rude to you. To a priest. But why should he be? He was as displeased with Andrew Pilsen as I was."

"Eunice had told him that I was for the marriage, that I was urging her into it though she was not sure."

Why did she not feel surprise? As soon as Father Dowling spoke, Zoe Flanagan recognized the crazy truth of what he was saying. Eunice had given exactly opposite stories to Bill and to her. She stared at Father Dowling.

He said, "She did tell me that you were opposed to the marriage."

"What is the boy like, Father?"

"I never met him."

"But weren't they coming to you . . . " She stopped. She sensed that it would be a difficult matter separating truth from untruth in what Eunice had told her. Eunice was a liar.

She had never admitted this to herself before, at least not quite so starkly, but it stated a simple truth about her daughter. Eunice was an incorrigible liar. She had lied when she was a little girl and she had been lying ever since.

"She didn't come home last night," she said bleakly.

"Does she live at home?"

"Now. She had an apartment, but I persuaded her to come home."

"Why?"

"There was no point in her living alone. God knows she does whatever she wants no matter where she lives. It just seemed awful, Eunice all alone in an apartment. She went to Rosary College," she added pointlessly.

"I see."

"Did she tell you that?"

"Doesn't Eunice work, Mrs. Flanagan?"

"Yes. For Morrissey and Morrissey. She answers the phone!"

"Why don't I telephone there then. Wouldn't that be reassuring?"

"Yes, Father. Please."

He looked up the number and dialed it as she sat watching him. He must think her an idiot. Why hadn't she called Morrissey and Morrissey? Several times she had dialed the number and then quickly hung up before it could be answered. Eunice hated being checked up on. Zoe had hoped her husband would call the lawyer's office to see if Eunice was there. Zoe removed her gloves and lay them on her lap. Pale blue, boneless hands, lifted in supplication. Her mother praying. She shivered. Father Dowling was waiting patiently, the phone to his ear.

"Hello. May I speak with Eunice Flanagan, please." A pause. "I see. Thank you very much."

"She's not there."

"You're not surprised, are you? Now there is nothing to be concerned about, Mrs. Flanagan. I don't know Eunice very well, but I know her well enough not to be surprised by the fact that she doesn't keep you fully informed on what she's doing."

Mrs. Flanagan nodded. She wanted reassurance, even if she did not believe it. He must know that it was not Eunice's physical welfare she was concerned about. Who was Eunice with? Where had she spent the night. *My evil abominable youth* . . . Zoe snatched up her gloves.

"Thank you, Father. You're very kind. I'm sorry to have taken up your time."

"Mrs. Flanagan, you're not interrupting me. This is why I'm here."

"We're not your parishioners."

He smiled. "I won't hold that against you."

She opened her purse and a pained expression formed on his face. He took her arm and led her down the hall. She had offended him. But no, he had already forgotten. He came with her onto the front stoop.

"Keep me informed, Mrs. Flanagan. And of course if I learn anything I'll let you know."

He made her feel less like a neurotic mother. Perhaps like her own mother, she should go home and pray. On her way to the car, she glanced at the church. But it would be ostentatious to go in there now. Father Dowling would think she was trying to impress him. At home she would kneel down beside her bed and pray for Eunice.

An odd thought occurred to her. Had her mother been praying for her?

What a pleasant idea! That old disturbing image altered. Her mother had been praying for her. Well, she thought, what else are mothers for?

29

AFTER Mrs. Flanagan had gone, Father Dowling returned to the parlor and opened the desk drawer. Inside was the index card on which he had written the information Eunice Flanagan had give him. Andrew Pilsen.

But it was not precisely Mrs. Flanagan's perspective that he took when his eyes lifted from the card and he looked reflectively out the window. He began to nod. Of course. Here was the way to put together the two events. A single target, Roger Dowling; and now a single enemy. If Eunice had told her parents conflicting stories of his attitude toward her projected marriage with Andrew Pilsen—would Wild Bill have been so angry at Roger Dowling's "grilling" his man Cowper if he did not believe Roger Dowling was encouraging Eunice to marry Pilsen?—what might she not have told the boy himself? Flanagan's fury on the phone had been that of a father who has lost control of his daughter far more than of an indignant employer, and it was a fury Eunice had deliberately provoked. Again Roger Dowling wondered if Andrew Pilsen were merely a figment of the girl's imagination.

The whole thing was rendered spongy by the fact that Eunice was obviously a pathological liar. Father Dowling had only her word for Pilsen's antireligious attitude. That might have been invented. Pilsen himself might be an invention.

He got out the phone book and was almost relieved to find Andrew Pilsen on the page, but then Mrs. Flanagan had said her husband had had him checked out. Having ascertained that Pilsen was indeed a real person was scarcely sufficient grounds for calling Phil Keegan. They had not spoken since the Chirichi episode and Roger Dowling knew how little his old friend enjoyed making a fool of himself, or even seeming to. Yet what had these past days been but a continuing humiliation for Phil? Being assaulted in the Dunbar house, chasing around after Chirichi's van only to find it empty. Of course police work was largely that, the disproof of theories, showing that something is not so. But there seemed no thread to the events of the past weeks. A random rifleman taking a shot, a shot that just happened to strike Billy Murkin? The kidnapping of Bishop Rooney.

Dowling got to his feet. He would not call Keegan. He still held the index card. He tapped his jaw with it several times, then left it on the desk blotter, tucking it in a corner. Hänsel and Gretel leaving a trail?

He had difficulty finding the address given for Andrew Pilsen in the phone directory. It took him into a warehouse area and he began to wonder if it was a misprint—had he ever discovered a misprint in the telephone directory? And then he saw the side stairway leading to a door very high up and toward the back of a warehouse. At the dock, several men were loading a truck and they paused in their labor.

"Can I do something for you, Father?"

"Can you tell me if that's an apartment up there?" He pointed. The man who had spoken had come to the edge of the dock and he followed Dowling's pointing finger. He took off his cap and wiped his forehead on his sleeve, giving the impression that it was summer rather than very early spring. "That used to be the watchman's place, Father. He lived there."

"Used to be?"

"They rent it out now."

"That's the place I'm looking for. Do you know Andrew Pilsen?"

"Who's he?"

"He rents that place."

"No, I wouldn't know him. We're just making a delivery, Father. The reason I know about that place, I knew the watchman."

"Well, thank you."

"Can you imagine living down here? Daytime, all right, but at night? Nothing but warehouses." The man shivered and fluttered his lips. "Spooky."

The stairs were metal see-through affairs and it was impossible to go soundlessly up them. They made a single diagonal line on the side of the building, stretching toward the high far door. It helped to keep his eyes on the door, but from time to time he looked down and saw the ground far below. His car was parked in a patch of sun. The trucker had said it would be spooky here at night. Roger Dowling found the area eerily deserted now. There were no signs of activity that he could see or hear.

The door, when he reached it, was steel, its little

window embedding wire octagonals. And dust. He put his face to the window and tried to see inside. If he could not see perhaps he would be seen. He tried the door. Locked. It was impossible not to look back down the long reach of stairs up which he had climbed. Vertigo. What an aerie! His grip on the railing tightened. From inside the door came a sound. Someone was working on the lock. And then the door began to open, very slowly. Suddenly it swung outward and Roger Dowling felt threatened by the great steel plane moving toward him, claiming the space of the landing on which he stood.

Eunice Flanagan looked out. Her eyes were wide, watchful, unsurprised.

"Come in, Father Dowling."

Inside was vaguely reminiscent of Chirichi's van, only on a far larger scale. A single large room with skylight, a bed against the far wall.

And on the bed, seated, a wan smile on his face, Arthur Rooney.

"Don't tell me you're in on this, Roger."

Dowling crossed the room quickly to Rooney and took his hand. It was a relief to find Rooney unruffled, almost dapper still. He was wearing his suitcoat, and his collar, though not quite as immaculate as it might be, rose beneath his chin as always. His smile, though forced, bore some resemblance to his usual happy countenance.

"Thank God, you're all right, Bishop."

"I think I complained to you about how dull my days are, Roger."

"What exactly happened?"

But Rooney nodded toward a television set whose image flickered cloudily. It was a street scene, a very large truck, its tailgate down. Men were handing cartons into the crowd that swarmed around the truck, hands reaching, reaching.

"Where is Pilsen?" Father Dowling asked Eunice. Having locked the door, she had come to look at the television.

"Do you know these people, Roger?"

"Eunice is an alumna of Rosary College, Bishop." For the first time, Dowling noticed that Rooney's ankles were hobbled with what looked like clothesline. "Where is Andrew Pilsen, Eunice?"

"He's at work."

"At work. Is this just a part-time occupation for him, kidnapping clergy?"

Dowling knelt down and began to untie the rope at Rooney's ankles.

"Don't do that."

He ignored her. Rooney laid a hand on his shoulder. "Better not, Roger."

Father Dowling turned. Eunice was holding a rifle and something in her vacant look suggested caution. Dowling rose.

"Eunice, the purpose of all this has been achieved. You can see that for yourself." He indicated the television. "There is no further point in holding Bishop Rooney."

"Is he really a bishop?"

"Yes."

"Andy will have to decide."

"Eunice, Andy is in very serious trouble. So are you. Let's not make it worse by prolonging it. If you let the bishop go before the police get here, it will go far easier for you."

"I haven't done anything."

"I'm glad to hear that. Now put down the rifle."

For answer, she lifted it and fired. A tremendous roar

and the sound of a slug above and then behind him, ripping through wood and metal.

"Sit down, Father Dowling." She prodded him with the smoking barrel of the gun. Roger Dowling sat side by side with Bishop Roone on the unmade bed.

"She is crazy," Rooney whispered.

"You may be right. When did the man leave?"

"Hours ago. They took my watch. They took my ring and pectoral cross too. Reduced to the ranks." Rooney smiled. "How did you know I was here?"

"A lucky guess. The girl had come to see me. She mentioned the man who lives here."

"Stop talking!"

"Eunice, your mother came to see me. She is worried about you."

"I don't care what that old bitch thinks."

This was a different Eunice from the girl who had sat, confused, in the rectory parlor.

"Get Andy on the telephone, Eunice. I want to talk to him."

"I said shut up."

The fact that she had already fired the rifle once was a cogent memory. Dowling fell silent and watched Eunice watch the television. How singularly joyless she was. If she had been looking forward to seeing half a million dollars' worth of food distributed, she clearly found the event itself disappointing. The announcer was saying that the archdiocese expected to be contacted soon by the kidnappers. Prayers were being offered for the safety of Bishop Rooney.

Rooney whispered, "At first they thought I was you."

"I know."

"I confess I wished I was."

"Oh?"

"I mean I wished that it was you they had. Not a very noble thought. Nobility and dignity are difficult to retain when you are being pushed and shoved about by a man with a rifle."

"How did it happen?"

"When I came downstairs, I stepped outside, intending to take a short walk. He was coming up the walk from the street."

"She wasn't with him?"

"Oh no. Just the man she calls Andy. She has only been here a few hours. In a way, she is more menacing than the man."

"You slept here?"

"Insofar as I did."

Eunice glared at them and they stopped talking. It was like being caught whispering in study hall back at Quigley.

The channel Eunice had been watching returned to regular programming and she twirled the dial looking for more faithful coverage of the food distribution and found none.

"I wouldn't mind having some of that food myself," Rooney said.

"Haven't they fed you?"

"I had a hamburger. What time is it?"

Dowling showed him. His watch read three o'clock.

"Thirty-two hours," Rooney said after a bit, still whispering. "I have decided that I would make a very poor martyr, Roger. I would give anything to get out of here."

Dowling glanced down at Rooney's ankles. He had loosened the knot in the rope, but that was all. Why had not Rooney bent over and untied the knot himself, for heaven's sake?

"The man fired a shot over my head too, Roger," he said, as if reading Dowling's thoughts. "Does anyone know you're here, Roger?"

Dowling shook his head.

"They don't mean to let me go, Roger. You really should not have come."

What Dowling regretted was having come alone. But even if he had had the intention to telephone Keegan once he located Pilsen's place, that long open stairway would have changed his mind. This was not a place that could be taken easily by force. Of course, his stupid vanity had been operative too. He had told himself that he knew Eunice and from hearing her talk of Andy he felt he knew Pilsen too. He would talk sense into them. Come, let us reason together. That nonsense had been knocked out of his head when Eunice fired a slug over it. Had her visits to the rectory been made with an eye to the kidnapping? Had Billy Murkin been the mistaken victim of the rifle Eunice now held?

Eunice had turned down the sound of the television but left the picture on. It began to flop over and over. However unintentional on her part, this was torture indeed. Anyone forced to watch that rolling picture, soundlessly turning, turning, would eventually come unhinged.

"Eunice, you must feed Bishop Rooney. He is hungry. He has had only a hamburger in thirty-two hours. Doesn't Andy keep food here?"

"I'm not cooking."

"You don't have to cook. There must be crackers, cookies, some milk."

"I don't have to do anything."

Dowling stood. "Of course you don't. I'll do it."

She did not object and he headed toward the corner of the room where there were cupboards, a sink, a stove, and refrigerator. He turned on the water and let it run. In the mirror over the sink, he saw with relief that Rooney was quietly, secretly untying the rope. Letting the water continue to run, he got the coffeepot from the stove. Having rinsed it out, he filled it with water, making as much diverting noise as he could. Coffee from the cupboard into the pot, the pot on the stove, the fire turned on.

"We can all use some coffee," he said to Eunice. She was watching him with fascination.

In the refrigerator were eggs, some cold meat, and a half-gallon carton of milk. Dowling took the milk from the refrigerator, glanced to see that Rooney was free, called to Eunice and tossed the milk carton to her.

The rifle clattered to the floor as her hands went up, to catch or fend off the tumbling milk carton. Roger Dowling stamped his foot on the fallen rifle.

"Go, Arthur. Now. Out the door and down the stairs. My car is parked just below. The keys are in it. Hurry."

Bishop Rooney scampered to the door, tugged twice, got it open and then was gone. Eunice had flung the milk carton away and, on her knees, was trying to pry the rifle free. Roger Dowling now had both feet firmly planted on it, one on the stock, the other on the barrel.

"You told me Pilsen worked nights," he said chidingly.

"He does."

"Where is he now?"

She looked up at him with hatred. "He wanted to get out of here. He was sick and tired of being holed up with that ridiculous man."

"When do you expect him back?"

Eunice turned away, toward the door. He had heard it too. The bonging sound of feet on the metal stairs. Coming up, not going down. They stopped. The door opened and

Bishop Rooney's crestfallen face appeared. He entered the room slowly and close behind, holding the bishop's arm painfully up between the shoulder blades, was a dissolute-looking young man who could only be Pilsen.

"He's got the gun," Eunice cried.

But the rifle was on the floor beneath Roger Dowling's feet and Pilsen claimed to be holding a knife at the bishop's back. Dowling stepped off the rifle and Pilsen rudely shoved Rooney away. The bishop stumbled but did not fall; his momentum carried him to the bed where he sat. Pilsen did not have a knife and Eunice snatched up the rifle. Pilsen approached Dowling, his smile triumphant, his manner contemptuous.

"You're Dowling, right?" Addressing Eunice but continuing to look at Dowling, he said, "You're right. They do look alike. It was an honest mistake."

"It was certainly a mistake," Dowling said.

The man slapped him, not hard. It seemed a symbolic blow. He slapped Dowling again, this time with the back of his hand.

"Stop that," Rooney cried.

Dowling would have liked to feel an evangelical tolerance, offering his cheek for Pilsen's striking, but anger flared in him and it was all he could do not to curse this insolent young man. The instinctive reaction must have shown in his eyes. Pilsen's smile broadened.

"Blessed are the meek."

Dowling gritted his teeth and managed to say nothing. If Rooney doubted his own capacity for martyrdom, Dowling felt less capable of the ultimate sacrifice. The bishop had managed to get through thirty-two hours with some semblance of aplomb whereas Dowling felt that, after two taunting slaps, he had revealed how thin the veneer of his virtue was.

"How did you guess the bishop was here?" Pilsen demanded.

"It didn't take much thought. I assume you are Andrew Pilsen."

"You assume right. What do you mean, it didn't take much thought?"

"Does it really matter?" The remark had been smug and he regretted it. But Pilsen would not let it go.

"It was a guess, that's all. Eunice's mother came to see me. She was worried about her daughter."

"Afraid she'd run away and married me?"

"She was worried. After she left, I recalled Eunice's speaking of you. She described you as someone who despises religion and priests."

"It's hypocrisy I despise."

"Pilsen, you've accomplished what you wanted. The food is being distributed right now. We saw it on television only minutes ago."

"I know. I caught some of it in a bar. I wanted to hear what people said while they watched."

"Were you gratified?"

Pilsen frowned. "Do you know most people resented it? Poor folks getting food for nothing and they resent it. They're mad at those people and they're mad at me." He shook his head. "No, I was not gratified."

On the stove the coffee boiled over.

"Get that, Eunice," Pilsen barked. She did, but she obviously did not like being ordered about.

"You can't know that those reactions are typical," Dowling said. "In any case, they are not Bishop Rooney's fault."

"They're typical. Take my word for it."

"You must let Bishop Rooney go. If you need a

hostage, I'll stay. You would have been satisfied with me yesterday morning."

"That was yesterday morning. You think I'm going to let him walk out of here and call the police?"

"He couldn't explain to them where we are. He doesn't know Fox River well. Drive him away from here and release him."

"No."

"Please."

Pilsen was surprised. "No, I can't."

"What do you intend to do?"

The insolence dissolved. Pilsen was a confused young man. Somehow that made him seem more dangerous than before. He looked at his watch. "I gotta go to work."

"And leave us with Eunice?"

Pilsen seemed to detect in the remark some nuance Rober Dowling had not intended. He looked at Eunice. She had poured a cup of coffee for herself and was now sipping it. Rooney could not conceal how much he would have liked a cup of coffee.

"You'll be okay alone. You'll never break out of here."

Dowling said, "The bishop has to eat. I'm going to fix something for him."

He was not stopped. The first thing he did was bring Rooney a cup of coffee. The bishop looked his thanks and brought the cup immediately to his lips. There was bread in the freezer. Dowling toasted several slices and made a sandwich with the cold meat. There was mustard but no lettuce. Did Pilsen eat no greens? He had a sallow look. Rickets, beriberi, worse? Dowling mentioned these legendary dangers and Pilsen sneered.

"Don't worry about me."

"I'm hungry too," Eunice said. She seemed to expect someone to feed her.

We'll be going," Pilsen assured her.

"You're going to work?"

"I have to. I don't want to create any suspicion."

"He left me alone last night too," Rooney said. He might have been reassuring Roger Dowling. Once more they sat side by side on the edge of the bed.

"Did you try to get out?"

"It's hopeless."

"But the phone?"

"He ripped the cord from the wall. Besides, I was completely tied up."

"We're going," Pilsen announced. He and Eunice had been whispering in the kitchen area and she now stood by the door, hitching the strap of her purse over her shoulder with one hand, the rifle dangling from the other. Dowling wondered which of them owned that rifle. Eunice seemed quite at ease with it. When she fired it earlier it had not seemed the first time she had done so.

"We'll stay," Dowling replied, striving for a cheerfulness he was far from feeling.

"That's right," Pilsen growled, looking at a watch, Rooney's watch. "It will be late when I get back. You needn't wait up."

Eunice left first. Pilsen looked back at them, seemed satisfied, and then the door closed. There was the sound of a key and, in a moment, the bonging sound of the metal steps growing ever fainter. It was the only outside sound that reached them and soon it was gone.

Dowling went back to the kitchen area. "Well, let's see what we have."

"Maybe you can find a way out of here," Rooney said hopefully.

"Right now I'm more concerned to get something to eat."

30

ALL MARIE MURKIN could tell him was that Father Dowling was out, he had not said where he was going.

"What time did he leave?"

"I'm not sure, Captain Keegan. He just went out."

"You didn't see him go?"

"There was someone here to see him. Mrs. Flanagan. Perhaps they went somewhere together."

But Mrs. Flanagan, when Keegan called her, sounded surprised that he should think that Father Dowling was with her. "We said good-by at the rectory door."

"Would your visit have prompted him to leave?"

A moment of silence. "I shouldn't think so."

"A confidential matter?"

"Yes."

She was indignant now and he did not blame her. Nonetheless, he felt that she was overreacting. No, that was

• 178 •

not true. He feared that it was he who was overreacting. He could not explain why he was concerned that Roger Dowling had left the rectory and Marie Murkin did not know where he had gone.

When the distribution of the food was being shown on television, Keegan again called to be told that Father Dowling had not returned.

"I'm going out there," he told Horvath.

"Want me to come along?" Cy looked awful. "I didn't keep a very good eye on him."

"How many jobs can you do? Come on along."

"Yeah."

His concern had been communicated to Marie Murkin and when they arrived at St. Hilary's, she let them in with a worried expression on her face. They went into the study where Keegan sat behind Dowling's desk. Marie, disapproving of such presumption, stood in the doorway.

"When did Mrs. Flanagan arrive?"

"Father Dowling answered the door. It was early afternoon."

"Did they talk here?"

"No. In the front parlor."

"Show me."

Once more Keegan sat at the desk where Dowling would have sat. Immediately his eye was drawn to an index card inserted in a corner of the desk blotter. Eunice Flanagan. Andrew Pilsen. He asked Marie who the couple was.

"Just that, a couple. I think it was marriage instructions."

"She's Mrs. Flanagan's daughter?"

"I guess."

This time, Keegan was less inclined to be apologetic when he got Mrs. Flanagan on the phone.

"I'm calling from Saint Hilary's rectory, Mrs. Flanagan. Father Dowling has not returned. I'm sure you're aware that there was a kidnapping from this house yesterday morning."

"What on earth . . ."

"Who is Andrew Pilsen?"

"He is a friend of my daughter."

"Are they getting married?"

"Captain, I hardly think that is any concern of the police."

"Where does he live?"

Silence. "I don't know."

"You don't know? Does he live in Fox River?"

"Yes, I think so."

"What kind of man is he?"

"I don't know," she wailed. "I've never met him."

"Is he a Catholic?"

She hung up. Keegan put down the phone. He held the index card in front of him. "Marie, does Father Dowling usually leave cards like this out?"

"Nooo." She did not think it important. Did he?

He got a telephone directory out of the drawer. Pilsen, Pilsen. He found it. Was it only his imagination that the book seemed to open easily to this page? He dialed the number. Nothing. He rang the operator. The number should be working. She would try it. But she could not get through either.

"There must be some malfunction, sir. We'll send someone out."

"Don't. This is Captain Keegan, Fox River police. I'll check it out and let you know."

"What do you make of this address?" he asked Horvath in the car. He had jotted it down from the directory before leaving.

"Can't be where he lives. That's all warehouses down there."

"You sure?"

"Positive."

Horvath was right. The streets were oddly deserted in the area at this hour of the late afternoon and they cruised along, not speaking, both sure there was something wrong. And then Horvath sat forward.

"Look. That's Dowling's car."

Keegan swung over to a loading dock and stopped. They got out quietly, leaving the car doors open. Approaching the priest's car stealthily, they converged on it quickly, running on the balls of their feet. The car was empty. Keegan looked around. Horvath was at the rear of the car, his ear pressed against the trunk. Keegan reached into the car and plucked the keys from the ignition. Roger should know better, he thought, but he could have cheered the presence of the keys. Horvath unlocked the trunk and stepped back. The door lifted slowly, eerily. Empty. Thank God.

Horvath now looked around. He pointed to a metal stairway that angled up the side of the warehouse. They ran to it. Keegan laid a hand on Horvath's arm and they looked up the lengthy rise of steps. It was more effective than a moat.

"Dowling's up there, Cy. I'm sure of it. The question is, who else is there?"

Horvath looked at him with disapproval.

"The bishop, Cy."

"Captain, you heard Mrs. Murkin. Marriage instructions. The future mother-in-law stops in for a chat. Father Dowling comes down here to talk to the guy."

"Just ordinary parish business?"

"Why not?"

"Want to go?"

"No."

Keegan sent Horvath reconnoitering, to see if there was any other access to the top floor where the stairway ended.

But the warehouse was locked, Horvath could find nobody. Did Keegan want him to break in? Phil Keegan looked up the stairs. "We'll go up this way."

As soundlessly as he could, Keegan crept up that flight of stairs. He had the sensation he was mounting some scary ride at a carnival. He hated heights. But his sense of relief was mixed when he got to the top. He raised himself from a crouch and brought his face against the cloudy window. Looking back at him, his face fragmented by the wire octagonals embedded in the glass, was Roger Dowling.

31

Two DAYS later Father Dowling ran into Flo Hanson in Kunert's Pharmacy. Bishop Rooney had gone off to Bermuda for a convention of diocesan social commissioners and was said to be recuperating on the beach and eating little. Roger Dowling's stomach was still queasy, apparently from what he had eaten in Pilsen's lair. He was browsing among the nonprescription counters in search of something that would keep the doctor away.

"Father!" Flo cried. "You're a celebrity."

"Rob a bank, Mrs. Hanson. You can be one too."

"You did nothing wrong."

"Well, be robbed then. Thank God everything turned out all right."

"How is Bishop Rooney?"

"I'm told he's mending." He did not add that he was accomplishing this under the Caribbean sun. The reticence was induced by the sight of Bunny Flynn bearing down on them.

"The confirmation was marvelous," Bunny assured Father Dowling.

"Thank you." Roger Dowling was not sure that he liked liturgical events to be rated like show biz, but a contented Bunny Flynn was preferable to the woman who had tried to persuade him of the desirability of reorganizing the parish into committees.

"Bishop Rooney is a wonderful man. But what a sequel! Being kidnapped, feeding all those people. Dick and I have a theory, Father." She drew closer and spoke in a stage whisper. "We think he arranged the whole thing, to pry money out of the cardinal."

"The cardinal made it clear that only the method, not the amount distributed, was influenced by the kidnapping."

Bunny Flynn gave him a look. They knew better.

"But, Father," Flo said. "How brave you were, going right down there where they were holding the bishop."

Brave? Other ways of describing it had occurred to him while he and the bishop had gone over the whole apartment in search of some way out other than the door. Rooney had called the place a fire trap, and the remark had not helped. More than ever, they had felt penned up there. What assurance did they have that Eunice and Pilsen would ever return? Finally, Dowling had found a small wrench under the kitchen sink and was preparing to go to work on the door window when Phil Keegan peered in at him.

It had taken two shots and a crowbar fetched by Horvath to get the door open, a fact that was not lost on Bishop Rooney.

"We could never have gotten out by ourselves, Roger."

"Oh, I don't know, Bishop. In a sense we did. It was our prayers that were answered."

Bunny Flynn said, "What will happen to that girl, Father?"

"I haven't any idea."

"Isn't it pretty clear that she was no more involved than Bishop Rooney or yourself?"

"Is it?"

"According to the paper, she was in the place only a few hours. Under threat by this Pilsen. And he took her with him when he left."

"She was his fiancée."

"That wasn't in the papers."

"I noticed that. Well, I've got to do some shopping."

They let him go and he picked up a bottle of Kaopectate as surreptitiously as he could. Passing the prescription counter, he was reminded of the overflowing medicine cabinet in the Dunbar bathroom. All those bottles and vials and tubes, most of which had come from Kunert's. He did not remember the name of the prescribing doctor but it would be typed on the labels.

"Yes, Father?"

The pharmacist was middle-aged, bald, and his wide blue eyes seemed not to need to blink. Perhaps he wore contacts. It was the odd man the pharmacist's age who did not wear glasses. On the breast pocket of his smock was a plastic name tag. Q. White. Another tag or label emerged from Dowling's memory.

"I've got it." He held up his bottle in explanation.

"Kaopectate. I can recommend it, Father.

"Oh, I've used it before."

White smiled. His upper lip lifted and caused a pouching under his eyes. His eyes did not get the smiling signal. They remained cold and distant. "I guess we've all needed something like that from time to time. Give my regards to Mrs. Murkin."

"Did you really mean that about the girl, Father?" Bunny Flynn was back. "That she was involved?"

"All I said was that she was the fiancée of the man."

"The poor girl."

"Yes."

"He could have talked her into it before she understood what was going on."

Roger Dowling recalling Eunice firing the rifle over his and Rooney's head, said nothing. They parted again and he went to the front of the store. While Harry Kunert was making change, Father Dowling looked back toward the prescription counter. He decided not to ask Harry about White. He was not quite sure what the question would be.

At headquarters, Keegan was brisker and more cheerful than Roger Dowling had seen him in days. Mervel and Ninian were emerging from Phil's office when Dowling arrived. When they saw the priest, they seemed to hesitate, each waiting for the other to decide, finally let it go, whatever it was. They had interviewed Father Dowling more than enough for all concerned. How much longer could they eke out stories on the kidnapping of the bishop?

"Wait until it occurs to them to link it with the

shooting of Billy Murkin," Keegan said when Dowling brought the question in to him.

"I thought you were skeptical of any connection."

Keegan rocked back in his chair. "The rifle belongs to the girl."

"It does!"

"Well, to her father. The point is it isn't Pilsen's. The only way they could have gotten it is through her. Rooney said that it was the same rifle Pilsen had when he showed up at Saint Hilary's that morning. The girl is in it up to her ears."

"Motive?"

Keegan folded his arms and looked across his desk. "You. Your hunch looks better all the time. Oh, maybe not you personally. It might have been any priest. She has a real, almost pathological, hatred of religion. Maybe diabolical. When we picked them up, she did all the talking. Spitting out her words. Even Pilsen looked a bit shaken by her vehemence. If she had already talked to Morrissey then, I would have taken it as an act."

"Then Morrissey is representing her?"

"Yes. And only her. Pilsen will get a court-appointed. Morrissey will go the psychiatric route. Rightly so, I think. What in the world did you say to her?"

"What do you mean?"

"Roger, she hates you. She is sorry she didn't shoot both you and Rooney when she had the chance."

Roger Dowling's memories of what he had said to Eunice Flanagan contained no explanation for such animosity.

"Roger, I think she may have taken that pot shot that killed Billy Murkin."

"Thinking he was me. Was that the rifle used?"

Keegan nodded. "As sure as those things usually are. Of course, we'll pin it on both of them."

"Have you mentioned the killing?"

"Not to her. After that first questioning, Morrissey moved in. I won't be surprised if I never get to talk to her again."

"And Pilsen?"

"He denies it, of course."

"Who has the court appointed to defend him?"

"Well, Hogan hasn't finished drawing up the charge yet. You know Hogan. Probably Tuttle."

"Tuttle!"

"Everyone else is gainfully employed. I guess you were right, Roger."

"About the shooting and kidnapping being linked?"

"You don't seem very happy."

It was not the sort of thing one was likely to feel elation about. He thought of Pilsen, hairy, resentful, scruffy. The poor devil. Had he taken on his hatred from Eunice or had they come together because their hatreds matched? He would have liked to talk to Pilsen, but he suspected that might make matters worse. Look how he had affected Eunice Flanagan, all unbeknownst. All priests are the same, as priests, but beneath that their manners and outlooks and characters differ enormously. Who was the right priest to get through to Pilsen? Ah.

"Phil, let Chirichi talk to Pilsen."

"Chirichi! What the hell for?"

"Why does any prisoner talk to a priest?"

"He hasn't asked for one."

"He'd see Chirichi. I'm sure he would."

"I wouldn't bet on it, Roger."

"Neither would I. But neither of us is a gambler. Chirichi is. That's how he won his van."

Keegan sighed. "How can I reach him?"

"Easy. Just tell Mervel that Pilsen has been asking for Chirichi."

"But he hasn't been."

"Okay. Tell Mervel that Pilsen has not asked for Chirichi. That should suffice for a story. And, if I know Chirichi, that will be enough for him too."

"You talk to Mervel. I just got rid of him."

Mervel, hat on the back of his head, a cigarette in his mouth, feet on the table, was paging through a glossy magazine when Father Dowling looked into the press room. Mervel got the magazine out of sight and scrambled to his feet. Dowling, looking sad, took a seat at the table, pulled out his pipe, studied its bowl, shook his head.

"What's the matter, Father?"

"Chirichi has not been given permission to see Andrew Pilsen."

"Why not?"

"Captain Keegan tells me that the prisoner has not asked for him."

"Has he?"

"I don't suppose it's a constitutional matter, exactly. Do you happen to know Tuttle's number?"

"Wait a minute. Let me get this straight. Pilsen wants to see Chirichi?"

"Not according to Keegan."

"Who told you, Chirichi?"

"He is a very difficult man to get hold of. You know that he lives in a van?"

"Priest prevented . . . no. Pilsen Prohibited Priest." Mervel took the cigarette from his lips, the better to appreciate the alliteration.

"I suppose *I* could insist on talking to Pilsen."

"No. We'll get Chirichi for him, Father Dowling. Don't worry about that. Even Pilsen has rights."

"But Pilsen hasn't asked to see Chirichi."

"According to Keegan?"

"According to Keegan."

"Can you imagine what the police think of a priest like Chirichi, Father?" Mervel, who had not sat down again, tipped his hat over his forehead. "I'll take care of this. Trust me."

Later that day, Father Dowling sat in his study in the rectory of St. Hilary's. His breviary was open on his lap, but he was not reading. His gaze seemed to be trained on a bookcase, but he did not see it. The name tag with its legend Q. White, like a stone in a stream, was causing eddies and swirlings he could not understand.

"Father?" Marie Murkin whispered his name from the doorway and he came alert. "I'm sorry to disturb you at your prayers, Father."

"You flatter me. I was daydreaming."

"Would you like a cup of coffee?"

"By the way, Marie. One of the druggists at Kunert's sent his regards. Mr. White."

"Quint?" Marie was blushing. "Honestly." She bent and began buffing the arm of a chair with the heel of her hand. "That needs polishing."

"Quentin White."

"He's not a Catholic."

"I didn't say he was."

"It's because of Billy, Father. His being dead." Marie paused and frowned. "It should affect me more, Father Dowling. But it doesn't."

"What about Billy?"

"Quint—Mr. White—said, well, now you're free. I thought he was kidding. It seemed in very poor taste anyway. But he didn't mean anything by it. Or so I thought. He wants to come calling on me." Marie threw up her hands and laughed, but the laughter became a kind of giggle.

"And has he come calling?"

"Would you mind if he did?"

"Why on earth would I mind?"

"It isn't as if I'm going to get married and leave you high and dry. He thought we might take in a movie and I said not during Lent so we'll just visit in the kitchen. He plays gin. You're sure you don't mind?"

"Marie, I'm delighted."

When she had gone off to get his coffee, the penny dropped. Quirk, B./White, Q. The tab on a dossier at the marriage tribunal. The two Q's. Quirk and Quentin. But that had been years and years ago. Quentin White and Blanche Quirk White Dunbar.

"Where are you going, Father?" Marie asked. She was holding a cup of coffee. Father Dowling, putting on his coat in the hallway, turned.

"I'm going into Chicago. Here, I'll have a sip of that. It looks chilly out."

"To Chicago at this hour? When will you be back?"

"Don't bother about supper, Marie."

"Don't bother? It's made. It's in the oven."

"I can't possibly get back in time."

"But all that food."

Dowling looked at her. "You could invite Mr. White to come share it with you."

"Maybe I will."

"Good-by, Marie."

The Quirk/White dossier had been begun almost twenty years before as an application for annullment by Blanche White née Quirk from Quentin White on multiple grounds. Quentin White had allegedly not had any intention of entering into matrimony because he had no intention of having children. This despite the fact that, verbally and in writing, he had agreed that the children of the union would be raised in the Church. Affidavits, letters, certificates, one a baptismal certificate testifying to Quentin White's reception of that sacrament, had been introduced. Clearly the Pauline privilege could not be invoked. As a baptized Christian, White would have entered into a sacramental marriage.

Leafing through the folder, seated in what had once been his office, Roger Dowling felt surrounded by ghosts, his own—memories of the years he had worked here assailed him, days filled with such cases as the Quirk/White one—and ghosts of this particular case. He had not been in on it during its heyday, but he recalled stories of the bitterness with which the matter had been pursued. It had been initiated in Peoria and been sent on to the archdiocesan tribunal. From the beginning, the husband had assumed that his wife's church would find some way to dissolve the marriage, something to which he was adamantly opposed. Whatever his wife's desire, it was clear he wished to remain her husband. There had never been the remotest chance of an annullment, nor was this merely a retrospective certainty. Any canon layer could have told from a glance at the dossier that the marriage of Blanche Quirk and Quentin White was valid and binding, that what God had put together no man might put asunder. No churchman, that is. If White grew more determined to keep his wife despite what he regarded as legal chicanery, Blanche was resolved to get out of the marriage one way or another. The sources of these tenacious cross purposes could only be guessed from the dossier. Ultimately Blanche had sought a civil divorce on grounds of mental cruelty and, although it was bitterly contested by White, it had been granted.

Then, silence. At least so far as the dossier went. It had remained here at the tribunal, a record of many many hours of work, gathering dust. Blanche was now dead, most of those who had given testimony or submitted affidavits were likely dead too. The evil that men do lives after them, in file cabinets, records, documents. Father Dowling closed the folder and sat for a while before returning it to the clerk.

He thought of a cluttered medicine cabinet filled with prescriptions from Kunert's Pharmacy where Mrs. Dunbar's first husband worked as a druggist, Quentin White of the odd eyes and odder smile who now wished to come calling on the first wife of James Dunbar, alias Billy Murkin. "Well, now you're free," he had said to Marie. The same might be said of him. Marie had been freed by a rifle shot. Mrs. Dunbar had died in a diabetic coma.

32

PHIL KEEGAN's apartment in Camelot Estates overlooked an artificial lake in which the lights of the buildings reflected cheerfully on this chilly night. Keegan slept here, he had at least breakfast in the apartment, but he did not really live there in any important sense. His life was his job as chief of detectives and it was almost with reluctance that he left his office at the end of the day He was never really unhappy when the day's task was prolonged. Now that he had Pilsen and the Flanagan girl locked up there was an inevitable lull and let down since there was little more for him to do. He was half sorry that he had let Cowper go. He could have bounced Leonard around a little more, given him a hard time. Instead he had gone off to dinner at an Italian restaurant, had two glasses of wine with his spaghetti, decided against going to the clubhouse of the Knights of Columbus: it was Ladies' Night and the place would be filled with female chatter. And so, he had gone unwillingly to his apartment, intent on going to bed early. Roger Dowling's phone call had come as a reprieve. Now, waiting for the priest to show up, looking out at the lights reflected in the artificial lake, Phil Keegan reflected on their friendship.

He had attended the seminary himself, had been in the class just behind Roger Dowling's, eventually had left. The service, intelligence work, discharge and the Fox River police. His wife was dead, his children lived elsewhere; he had not known how lonely he was until Roger Dowling had been assigned to St. Hilary's less than two years ago. Their shared past separated them as much as it linked them. Dowling discouraged Keegan's tendency to grow nostalgic about seminary life, assuring Phil that he had chosen the better part. "Look at what has happened in the Church, Phil. It would have driven you crazy."

Remembering that remark now, thinking of Chirichi, Keegan could only agree. Chirichi had shown up, demanding to see Pilsen, and had been visibly disappointed when he was waved right through to the cell block. Keegan, expecting Pilsen to demand that the suspended priest be thrown out of there, was surprised to hear that the two had gotten along famously. Chirichi had probably told Pilsen that he had shown genuine religious faith by kidnapping the bishop. If Chirichi could convince himself that he was still in the Church, he should not find it hard to include Pilsen as well.

Roger was right. If it were not for St. Hilary's and the traditional services conducted there, life would be a good deal more annoying for Phil Keegan than it was.

Dowling had telephoned from Chicago, but he should be here by now. It was unlikely that he would have been caught in a traffic jam at this hour. And then came the sound of the bell and Phil Keegan opened his door to Roger Dowling.

"Here, let me take your coat."

"I'm hoping to persuade you to come out."

"Where?"

"The Dunbar house."

"What for?"

"I'll tell you on the way."

"Uh uh. That place is a jinx. And it's become like Grand Central Station. We have sealed it tight and there are patrols keeping a close watch on it. I'm not going there unless I have to."

"Well, of course you don't have to come along."

"Roger, take off your coat and explain to me why you want to go there."

But Dowling opened the door. "I'll come by again after I've been to the house. I would have stopped there on my way . . ."

"All right. All right. Wait a minute. I'll go with you."

They had to stop by headquarters for keys and they ran into Horvath there. Keegan asked him to follow along in another car.

"What are we after?"

"Wild geese. I've been rapped on the head, Father Dowling has been held hostage. It's your turn, Cy. Maybe something nice will happen to you this time."

"What are we after?" Horvath repeated, undeterred by Keegan's uncharacteristic sally.

"Ask Father Dowling."

"It shouldn't take but a minute, Cy," Father Dowling said.

A minute after they had entered the house and turned on lights, a patrol car arrived, alerted by Mrs. Wenzel next door. Horvath assured the officers everything was fine. Dowling had headed immediately for the stairway and Keegan followed him up. In the bathroom, Roger opened the medicine cabinet. There was a look of acute disappointment on his face.

"I was afraid of this."

"What's wrong?"

"It's empty."

"I can see that."

"Don't you remember the way it was the other day? It was chock-full."

Keegan was not sure that he remembered that. He did remember Roger not finding any aspirin in the medicine cabinet.

"There's medicine in the bedroom too, Roger."

Dowling brushed past him. But the bottles and jars on the dresser did not interest him. Keegan was getting peeved.

"What are you looking for?"

"For what isn't here. Who cleaned out the medicine cabinet, Phil?"

"I don't know. I can find out."

Horvath had joined them and now said, "I have a suggestion on where to start looking. You remember the wallet Cowper dropped when he was arrested and his story about an intruder in the house? We've traced the name in the wallet. Robert Fletcher. He lives in Peoria, near it, anyway."

"Bob Fletcher?"

Horvath looked at Dowling. "Do you know him?"

"Well, I know who he is. He's Marie Murkin's brother."

"What the hell was he doing snooping around this house?"

"I don't know, Phil. Why don't you ask him?"

"Have him extradited from Peoria?"

Dowling grinned. "He's in Fox River. He's staying in a motel."

"Which one?"

"Marie would know."

"Let's call her."

"No. Why don't we go to the rectory? I really should check in."

It hardly seemed a reason to make the trip, but Keegan liked Marie Murkin well enough not to want to disturb her with inquiries about her brother over the phone. At the house he would be nonchalant, he decided, settling in beside Horvath. We found your brother's wallet, how can we return it? Something like that.

"Where's Father Dowling?" Horvath asked, looking in the rear-view mirror. "He's not behind us."

"He knows the way home, Cy. Don't worry about it."

33

ROGER DOWLING let Horvath get half a block ahead before cutting his lights and pulling to the curb. A minute later, he turned on his lights and pulled away. His first need was a phone and he saw one almost immediately, an outdoor booth. But it was a shambles when he got to it. Someone had systematically pulled all the pages from the directory. Father Dowling returned to his car and drove to a restaurant wherein he assured the hostess he did not want a table.

"I have to telephone," he whispered.

"The rest rooms are down the hallway, sir," she said frostily.

"I really meant the telephone."

It was dark in the vestibule and he had difficulty reading the fine print. There were columns of Whites. Thank God for the distinctive first name. He jotted down the address.

He had no idea where it was. And so, emerging from the restaurant, he went to a cab waiting at the curb, settled in the back seat and gave the address for Quentin White he had just found in the telephone directory.

As he rode, he gave his pocket a confirmatory pat. The keys Phil had picked up at headquarters were a set meant to gain entrance almost anywhere. Father Dowling did not anticipate any difficulty at the apartment. White himself, he had to assume, was still at St. Hilary's rectory where, after having dined with Marie, he might even now be paying court to her. Roger Dowling felt that he had gained some understanding of Quentin White's interest in Marie Murkin. They were linked through their first spouses. And they had other things in common.

White lived in a housing development that overlooked the Interstate, the buildings wooden, of odd angular shapes, automobiles everywhere. The curbs were lined with them, parking lots were filled with them. To live in this development without a car would be to be stranded indeed.

"This the place, Father?" The cabbie's question seemed to contain another question.

"Fine. Good." Dowling reached for his wallet. "Can you wait for me? It shouldn't be long."

"Well, I don't know, Father."

"Just five minutes."

"Five minutes I can wait."

"Good." Dowling hopped out and headed toward the building. He hoped that he could accomplish what he came for in five minutes. But the driver would wait for his fare. Apartment 3D. An open stairway. Bicycles, wagons, trikes. There must be lots of kids. A thought struck him and made him stop. He had just assumed that White lived alone.

At 3D, he knocked and began to try keys in the lock.

Almost immediately he found one that fit. He knocked again, waited, then opened the door. The sound of music. He froze. No other sound. He stepped inside and closed the door softly behind him. He put the keys in his topcoat pocket and went toward the music. It was a kitchen radio, playing in the empty apartment. It was a one-bedroom apartment, three rooms in all, small and cheerless. How lonely it must be to sit here with the sound of children playing outside. And the roar of the Interstate. How close the highway was.

The kitchen light had been on. There was a plastic trash can next to the back door. Dowling removed the cover. It was filled with plastic bags, wound tight at the neck with a wire twist. But nestling among the bags were bottles, medicine bottles, many of them. He held one up to the light. The prescription had been made out to Blanche Dunbar. Her doctor was a man named Farber. Dowling took two of the bottles, one full, one half full, put the cover back on the trash can and hurried through the apartment.

As he descended he heard footsteps coming up the stairs. Feeling hypocritical, he adopted a somber expression. A priest out on his sad errands.

"Father Dowling! Is that you?"

Dowling peered at the man, but he had recognized the voice. "Good evening."

"I've just come from your house," White said, almost jovially. "What brings you here?"

"A priest's work is never done." He half expected a judgmental thunderbolt to issue from the night sky.

"But this isn't Saint Hilary's parish, is it?"

"No. And I must get back to it. Did you have a nice evening with Mrs. Murkin?"

"Indeed, indeed. She is a wonderful cook. You are a lucky man, Father."

"At least until she leaves."

"Where is she going?" White seemed alarmed.

"Well, after all, an attractive widow . . ."

"Ho, ho. I see what you mean."

"Well, good evening."

They shook hands and Father Dowling continued down. The touch of Quenten White's hand seemed impressed on his own. Roger Dowling was perspiring. Had he actually been afraid? The cabbie was pleased to see him again so soon. Dowling asked to be returned to the restaurant where he had left his car.

"Without the collar, I wouldn't have done it, Father. People do that. You know, wait for me, I'll be right back and I sit waiting and they never show."

"You should ask to be paid first."

"Right. That's the rule. But you were off and running before I could tell you."

"I'm sorry."

"I figured, a priest, how do I know what you're here for, know what I mean?"

"I appreciate it."

He appreciated it more when he was back in his own car and headed for St. Hilary's rectory. He hoped that Phil Keegan was still there.

"Cy find you?" Keegan asked.

"Find me?"

"We figured you ran out of gas or something. Where've you been?"

"Father," Marie Murkin said. "They found Bob's wallet. Isn't that amazing?"

"For heaven's sake," said Father Dowling.

"I can drop it off where he's staying, Marie," Keegan said.

"The Clover Motel. Where was the wallet found?"

"It was turned in." Keegan was seated at the kitchen table, a bottle of beer before him.

"How was your date, Marie? Father Dowling asked.

"Date?" Keegan looked at the housekeeper. "What's this?"

For answer, Marie Murkin began to blush.

Dowling said, "What time did he leave?"

"Just as Captain Keegan arrived."

"Did you meet him, Phil?"

"I met a man. A Mr. White. I had no idea he was Marie's beau."

"Oh, you two are awful. Get out of my kitchen."

And they did, with Marie assuring them she had not meant it. In the study, Keegan turned to Dowling "Where were you?"

Dowling took one of the medicine bottles from his pocket, the half full one, and shook several tablets into his hand. "Could you have those analyzed at the lab?"

"What for?"

"Just to see what they are."

"What are they supposed to be?"

"Insulin."

"Where did you get them?"

"Why don't I keep that a secret until the lab has made an analysis? If they're insulin, it will be simply something to forget."

Marie appeared in the doorway, carrying Phil's beer. "You didn't finish this."

"I was just about to go to your brother, to give him his wallet."

"You don't have to," Marie said, pleased with herself. "He is coming here."

34

TUTTLE had feared this ever since Robert Fletcher had come to him with the story of his entry into the Dunbar house. He had kept his ear to the ground at police headquarters but in all the excitement about the kidnapped bishop there was not much to hear. He bought Peanuts a chocolate ice cream cone in the lobby of the courthouse and said it was a damned shame about the hood of Horvath's car but Peanuts had just licked on.

"I meant the dent."

"What dent?"

"In Horvath's car." He inhaled. "The hood."

Peanuts laughed. "Horvath's no hood."

There went a wasted cone. Ah well. Tuttle chalked it up to keeping Peanuts friendly. After all, Peanuts had directed Bob Fletcher to him. Assuming that was a favor. Fletcher had not mentioned losing his wallet in the fracas and now, on the telephone, he sounded nervous.

"They want you downtown?" Tuttle asked.

"No. Saint Hilary's rectory. My sister is housekeeper there."

"I thought you said that the police had your wallet which you lost breaking into Dunbar's."

"The police are at Saint Hilary's."

"I don't follow you."

"The police are there and they have my wallet. My sister told them I'd come and pick it up."

"Jesus Christ,' Tuttle said.

"You better not talk that way at the rectory."

"You want me to come with you?"

"I wish you would."

Tuttle thought about it. He liked a client who had the good sense to rely on counsel. It would take a level head to keep this from being blown into something serious. He told Fletcher he would meet him at St. Hilary's.

"Wait outside until I get there. I'll do the talking."

"What do you suppose they're up to?"

Good question, Tuttle thought, on his way to St. Hilary's. If worse came to worst, he would plead his client for breaking and entering. No need to mention the insurance policies. And even if they did come up, it was not as if Fletcher were seeking to deprive the rightful owner of his property. Fletcher's sister was the legal beneficiary, or would be as soon as Tuttle argued the case. The little lawyer whistled as he drove. Something Peanuts had said today made him feel happy despite this unscheduled activity for Fletcher. The rumor was that Tuttle would be appointed to defend Andrew Pilsen. Peanuts was sure he was sure. He asked Tuttle if he was surprised. The intrepid lawyer denied surprise. Pilsen was in big trouble. He would have need of counsel who feared no man, neither churchman nor politician, rich man or poor.

The tune he was whistling was *Dixie*.

35

WHEN FLANAGAN called him in, Cowper feared that Wild Bill
had heard of the second arrest, but when he entered the den of
the Flanagan home and found the boss huddled at the desk in
a little puddle of light that came from the lamp before him,
the only light on in the room, he knew it was something more
serious.

"The stuff isn't in the house," Flanagan said. "We
have to accept that."

"I'd like to give it one more sweep."

"You stay away from there. If it was there, you would
have found it by now, or someone else would have."

"Maybe it never will be found. How many people
would know what it was?"

Flanagan looked at him impatiently. "Are you
through developing stupid theories?"

"You want to just forget about it?"

"I want that material. I assume it is not in the house. Where is it?"

Cowper frowned in thought. "The bank? It could be in the bank."

"And it could be buried in a coffee can in the backyard."

Flanagan was kidding but Cowper was not so sure Wild Bill was wrong. He felt bad about not telling Wild Bill about the guy he had caught in the house. Fletcher. What would Flanagan do if he knew there were others anxious to get what was in the house? The hell with it. Let Flanagan figure it out for himself. Apparently Wild Bill thought he had done just that. He sat forward.

"I know where the stuff is. Don't ask me how I know. It's a hunch and I'm sure. I got rich playing my hunches."

It was Cowper's turn to stare. Wild Bill had got rich underbidding his competitors on the basis of information stolen for him by James Dunbar. If that was his idea of a hunch, Cowper was not interested in where Wild Bill thought Dunbar had stashed the incriminating evidence.

"Where did he die?" Flanagan asked.

Cowper scowled. "You know where he died."

"Right. Saint Hilary's rectory. Why?"

" 'Cause that's where he was when he got shot."

"Visiting his first wife, as we now know."

"Yeah." Flanagan's previous hunch had been that a grief-stricken Dunbar was going to make a clean breast of it to the priest. From that it would be only a baby step to talking to the police.

"He was in the housekeeper's bedroom when he was shot."

"So?"

"What was he doing there? I've learned something about that rectory. The housekeeper's room is on the second floor. That was in the newspaper. It is reached by a back stairway. It is just a little room. She can't entertain people there."

"Her husband?"

"That's where Dunbar hid the stuff, Cowper. I'm sure of it."

"You may be right."

"We'll soon know."

"How?"

"You're going to find out. Tonight. I want that room searched."

Cowper protested, of course he protested. His luck in entering homes uninvited was awful lately. But he knew that protesting would do him no good. Wild Bill had made up his mind. He did not give a damn how Cowper got in or out; he wanted that room searched from floor to ceiling.

"Chances are it's in some obvious place. But somewhere she won't have noticed."

"She would have found it."

But Wild Bill was full of certitude tonight. Which meant that he was scared too. When in doubt, do not doubt. Flanagan came to the door with him, which was a nice touch. They even shook hands, something they almost never did.

"Mr. Flanagan, let me get rid of that rifle. I could take it along now."

Wild Bill just shook his head.

"Why not?"

His hand closed on Cowper's arm.

"The police already have it."

36

KEEGAN had not been prepared for Tuttle, but then he seldom was.

The little lawyer entered the room first, shoulders back, belly out, chin tucked in. And talking. He was followed by a shy lanky man in denims who smiled sheepishly at Marie and then kept his eyes on his boots.

"My client is here to collect his wallet, gentlemen. He did not report its theft, but of course he is under no statutory obligation to do so. Besides a driver's license, social security card, membership cards in the Legion, Knights of Pythias, and Teamsters Union, there was a total of eighteen dollars in cash. Among the credit cards there was an American Express, a Standard Oil, a Sears, a Penney's . . ."

"Tuttle, since when does a man need a lawyer in order to claim lost property?"

"My client and I were in consultation when the call came. Isn't this a rather peculiar location for Lost and Found? Hello, Father Dowling. I am not sure that we have met, but naturally I recognize you from your picture in the paper. A harrowing experience. Harrowing. Give my best to the bishop when you see him. Horvath?" Tuttle glanced at Bob Fletcher who, having looked at Horvath, shook his head. Tuttle's professional frown gave way to a beaming smile. "And this is your sister?"

"Hello, Mr. Tuttle," Marie said. "We already met in your office."

Keegan found this intriguing. "Is Mr. Tuttle your lawyer, Marie?"

"I guess so. I've never had a lawyer before."

"I represent both Mrs. Murkin and her brother Mr. Fletcher. Now, where is the wallet?"

Keegan took it from Horvath and examined it. Cowper had had it with him when he was arrested in the alley behind the Dunbar house. His claim was that he had taken it from a man who had been inside the house. Cowper's description, insofar as Keegan could remember it, matched Bob Fletcher.

"What were you doing at the Dunbar house, Mr. Fletcher?"

"Now just a minute, Captain," Tuttle said. "What is the Dunbar house?"

"Dunbar is the name that Mrs. Murkin's husband had been living under," Father Dowling said. "Look, why don't we all sit down. Marie, is there coffee for your brother and Mr. Tuttle?"

Marie continued to look at her brother. "Yes, Father."

"Your sister's husband's house," Keegan said to Fletcher. "No kids, no relatives. None, that is, except Marie, so far as I know. I suppose a case could be made that the Dunbar house is your sister's now. Is that the way you figure it?"

"That's the way I figure it." These were Fletcher's first words.

"A case not only could be made, it will be made," Tuttle announced.

"The house, and I suppose everything else, would go to Marie."

"Not would, Captain. Will."

"You may be right, Tuttle. Is that why you were in the house, Fletcher?"

"I didn't say I was in the house."

"Oh, Bob," Marie cried. "Stop it. They know you were there. Is that where you lost your wallet?"

Tuttle sent up a barrage of words, Fletcher tried to say something, not to Keegan but to Marie. Keegan did not catch what it was. Marie was weeping, embarrassed that her brother should be the center of this kind of attention.

"Not another word," Tuttle ordered.

"Mr. Tuttle," Marie shouted. "Will you please shut up? These people are my friends. I know them a good deal better than I do you and I won't have you butting in every-time something is said." She turned to Father Dowling, then to Keegan. "Captain, Bob and I went to see Mr. Tuttle in his office. He was recommended to Bob by someone downtown."

"Peanuts," Bob said.

Horvath groaned.

"Bob thought what you just said. If Billy had left anything, even under a false name, it could become mine. Mr. Tuttle thought so too."

"What sort of things?"

"Retirement benefits, insurance. Mainly insurance."

'How much insurance is there?"

"Plenty," Fletcher said.

Tuttle put his face in his hands.

"Is that what you took from the house the day you lost your wallet?"

Fletcher glanced at Marie. "Yes."

"And who has those policies? Tuttle?"

Tuttle bounded from his chair. "That is libelous. I had nothing to do with gaining control of those papers and they certainly are not in my possession."

"Do you have them, Mr. Fletcher?"

"No, I don't."

"Then where are they?"

Fletcher inhaled, looked again at Marie, and said, "Upstairs."

"Upstairs?"

"In Marie's room."

Keegan turned to Marie. She was obviously surprised. Fletcher went on.

"I put them up there, Marie. For safekeeping. I got them for you. I didn't want to leave them with Tuttle. He had a safe, but so what? I put them between the mattress and box spring of your bed."

Keegan said, "Go get them, Marie."

Marie looked around, as if to say that this was all news to her, then wheeled and went swiftly up the stairs. A silence fell over the rectory kitchen. The second hand on the electric clock above the stove moved 180° before Marie screamed.

It was a piercing scream and seemed to be amplified as it traveled down the stairway. Horvath got to the stairs first. Keegan was right behind him. They raced up the stairs to find Marie in her bedroom, hands raised in terror, backed against a wall. In the center of the room, a wild look on his face, a look of panic, of frustration, of doom, stood Leonard Cowper.

"I can explain," he cried to Horvath and Keegan.

He did not resist when Horvath snapped on the handcuffs.

"Three times and out, Cowper," Keegan said. "Your career as a second story man is over."

Keegan took hold of a corner of the mattress and lifted. There were half a dozen colorful folded documents there, obviously insurance policies. There was a manila envelope too. It was plain, except for a printed legend in the upper lefthand corner. Flanagan Construction. And the address. Making an animal noise, Cowper lunged for it, using both his manacled hands. Keegan let him hug it to his breast. Cowper made a feint toward the stairway, but that was now clogged with the others coming up from the kitchen. He would have had even less of a chance going for the open window.

"So that's what you were looking for, Leonard. Give it here."

"I'll clear the room if you want to talk to him here, Captain."

"No, Cy. Take him downtown."

"What's the charge?"

When Phil Keegan spoke, his voice was heavy and sad. "Murder," he said. "The murder of Billy Murkin."

37

It was nearly a week later that Phil Keegan came for dinner and was able to tell Roger Dowling what had been going on in the interim. The interim being Holy Week, Father Dowling had been extremely busy and had had little time to think about anything other than parish affairs. Marie of course relayed to him the news that no charges would be brought against her brother Bob, but that was the extent of Dowling's contact with the events of previous weeks. Now, Lent over, a sumptuous Easter dinner before them on the table, Marie kibbitzing as they ate, Father Dowling was glad to be brought up to date.

"Industrial espionage," Keegan said. "It's like any other kind of spying, I guess. You steal the other guy's secrets so he can't use them against you. Submitting sealed bids is less of a gamble if you know in advance what the contents of the other sealed bids will be. Flanagan knew. He got all the jobs he really wanted and he was smart enough to lose once in a while."

"Who was the spy, Cowper?"

"If he had been, Flanagan would have gone broke. Cowper was caught three times inside of a week. No, it was Dunbar."

"Billy Murkin."

"Who turns out to be loaded, Father." Keegan looked up at Marie who was presenting a bowl of sweet potatoes. "If you get that money, you're going to be a merry widow, Marie."

She made a face, but one that included a little smile. "Mr. Tuttle is optimistic."

"If you really want that money, you should change lawyers."

"Can I do that?"

"Of course. You may have noticed that Tuttle is not exactly effective."

"He got Bob off."

"He what!" Keegan sat back.

"He persuaded the police to drop all charges against Bob."

"Did he tell you that?"

"Well, he told Bob."

"It's not true, Marie. That decision was made by . . . by others. And believe me, Mr. Tuttle had absolutely nothing to do with it. His telling you that is reason enough to get rid of him. Tell it to your brother."

"Bob's gone back to Peoria."

"Good for him. Drop Tuttle, Marie."

Marie brought the bowl of potatoes to Father Dowling. Helping himself, Roger said, "About the spying. Why did they have to get rid of Dunbar?"

"He decided to make his efforts pay twice. That envelope contained proof that Flanagan had been using stolen data against his competitors for years. Dunbar was blackmailing him with the threat to turn him in."

"And Cowper was ordered to get rid of him?"

"That's right. He followed him here. Apparently he tried to get a bead on him several times but then when Billy went upstairs, Cowper went around the back of the house and he had to keep going in order to get a clear shot. He had to go all the way to the ramp of the freeway."

Marie had left the room so no terrible memories were stirred in her by Keegan's remarks. Father Dowling sipped his water. "But wasn't the rifle you found in Eunice Flanagan's car the one used to shoot Billy Murkin?"

Keegan nodded. "Do you know Flanagan?"

"Tell me about him."

"He is what his friends would call a bastard. God knows what his enemies call him. But underneath it all, he is a father. It is his testimony that saves Eunice, and Pilsen, from a murder charge. I don't know what he would have done if we hadn't caught Cowper and found that envelope. Would he have let Pilsen go to trial for shooting Billy as well as for kidnapping the bishop?"

"I doubt it," Father Dowling said. Phil had touched on something important. There are ultimate building blocks and paternity is one of them; it is a biological fact and a moral predisposition too. Flanagan would have found it too hard to permit his daughter to be accused of a murder he had ordered committed, and thus had committed himself, even if she could plead insanity.

"I hope you're right. Anyway, I think it's lucky he never had the choice. Cowper sang like a bird. He seemed under some compulsion to talk, to tell us how bad at his job he had been, as if that somehow excused him."

"I wish he had been worse at it the night he shot Billy Murkin. Do you suppose that was Billy's motive for the big reunion, a safe hiding place for his blackmail material?"

Keegan shrugged. "He must have known they'd be after him."

"Don't suggest that to Marie."

"Of course not."

For fifteen minutes they gave their undivided attention to the feast Marie had prepared. Father Dowling had urged her to join them this Easter day, but she refused as she always did.

Later, in the study, Keegan lit a cigar and Father Dowling filled his pipe. When he had it lit, he puffed in silence.

"Have you been following spring practice?" Phil asked.

"This could be the Cubs' year."

"If young Wrigley doesn't sell the whole team."

As it will with Cub fans, one remark led to another, and it was possible to believe that the day was not distant when they would be seated once more in the beloved park on the north side watching a team that rarely earned the devotion and loyalty showered upon it.

That topic dropped, if not exhausted, Keegan said, "Funny thing. Chirichi has really gotten through to Pilsen."

"Good."

"I'm told they're thick as thieves. Pilsen is quoted as saying that if he had met Chirichi sooner he would never have kidnapped Bishop Rooney."

"He'd have gone for the cardinal?"

"Who told you?"

"I guessed."

"Great minds."

"Hmm."

In the ensuing silence, their minds turned to the same thing. It was the information Dowling had dreaded.

"They weren't insulin tablets, Roger."

"I was afraid of that."

"Tell me what it means."

"You must have checked Mrs. Dunbar's death certificate."

"She died in a diabetic coma."

"Small wonder. What were those tablets?"

"Placebos."

"Ironic. Do you know what it means?"

"It's Latin, isn't it?" It had been the intricacies of that classic tongue that explained, at least in part, Phil Keegan's departure from the seminary years ago. He spoke petulantly.

"Yes. It means, I will please. What would you call giving a diabetic a worthless placebo instead of insulin?"

"What made you suspect it?"

Father Dowling knew that Phil was not asking why he had suspected foul play in Mrs. Dunbar's death. Phil knew that anyone is capable of anything. Roger Dowling's suspicion had begun as a thought about Billy Murkin. Had he eased his second wife into the next world in order to open the way to reconciliation with Marie? After Billy was dead, it would have been mere curiosity to pursue the thought. There was nothing to be gained from answering the question one way or the other. But once he had seen Quentin White in Kunert's Pharmacy, it had been another matter. Not that he had understood at first why White's name tugged at his memory. When he did understand, the old dossier at the marriage tribunal, its pages nearly twenty years old, still giving off the aroma of hate, suggested that Quentin White would not easily reconcile himself to the loss of his wife.

His wife had acquired anonymity by moving to Fox

River and marrying Billy Murkin, much as Billy had become anonymous by becoming James Dunbar. How had White tracked them down? Unlike Marie, he must have been in search of his lost spouse over the years and, when at last he found her, he had the perfect way to effect his revenge. He would deprive James Dunbar of a wife and his wife of her life by making her necessary medicine an instrument of death rather than health.

"It would be difficult to prove, Roger."

"You have the bottle from which the tablets came."

"Stolen by White from the Dunbar medicine cabinet?" Phil mused.

But Roger Dowling had little interest in what must interest Phil Keegan now: the amassing of the grist with which to feed the mills of justice. Another perspective took first place now. Dowling thought of Quentin White, nursing his hatred down the years. There was a perverted nobility in such dedication to a goal. And now the goal had been achieved. His enemy, his wife, was dead. What filled his soul now that it was drained of the determination to kill? *Post homicidium triste?* There was room for God and grace now, room for mercy.

"I'd like to have a talk with him, Phil."

"I don't know when we'll be ready to make an arrest. If ever. Let's face it, Roger. The man could get away scot-free."

"Oh, not as free as all that, Phil."

He did not have to wait for an arrest or any mediation by Keegan in order to have a talk with Quentin White. Two days later, the bell rang and Marie went to answer it. When he heard the voice, Father Dowling put a finger in the book he was reading and sat forward in his chair. Marie's face was flushed when she looked in. "Mr. White wants to talk with you, Father."

"Of course."

Quentin White came in, tall, bald, eyes wide and piercing, and Father Dowling could see that there would be no need for preliminaries. He indicated a chair.

"You were in my apartment that night we met on the stairs, weren't you, Father Dowling?"

"Why would I want to be in your apartment?"

"You found something in my trash that interested you."

"How do you feel, now that you have brought it off?"

"Do the police know what you took?"

"Yes."

White sighed. His arms rested on the arms of his chair, his hands hung limp. "I suppose it is only a matter of time."

"That could be a definition of life itself."

"So it could."

"You must pray for her now, Quentin."

"Pray for her!"

"Yes. How much, and how long, you have loved her. A love gone wrong, but still love of a sort. She is at peace now, we can hope. She will be praying for you."

White seemed to have difficulty deciding whether Father Dowling was serious. "If it had been left to your Church, I never would have lost her."

"You never did."

Thus a beginning was made. Roger Dowling felt certain their conversation would have a sequel, whether or not White was arrested for murder or some lesser offense, whether justice was done or not. Mercy would have its opportunity.

Bunny Flynn came to see him, bringing her husband Dick, and Father Dowling heard more than he wanted to hear of what parish life was like in Whichawa. He suspected Mr. Flynn was less enthralled by these memories than Bunny was. But the encouraging thing was that neither of them seemed to see any relation between their tales of liturgical derring-do and what went on in St. Hilary's parish in Fox River, Illinois.

Bishop Rooney telephoned when he returned from Bermuda where he had had a lovely restorative stay. He regretted he had not been there on the memorable occasion when Roger Dowling stopped by the marriage tribunal. Was Roger by any chance interested in returning to his old post?

"No, Bishop Rooney. Not in the least. I am perfectly content where I am."

"You have an interesting parish."

Interesting? It was not the adjective he would have chosen, but his reply was nonetheless fervent.

"Amen," Roger Dowling said. "Amen."